Butcher Boy Rebellion

Robert H Cherny

Published by Robert H Cherny, 2025.

This is a work of fiction. Similarities to real people, places, or events are entirely coincidental.

BUTCHER BOY REBELLION

First edition. February 15, 2025.

Copyright © 2025 Robert H Cherny.

ISBN: 979-8230870883

Written by Robert H Cherny.

Butcher Boy Rebellion
Robert H. Cherny
All rights reserved
Copyright © 2020 by Robert H. Cherny
This book may not be reproduced in whole or in part without written permission.
This book is a work of fiction. Any resemblance to actual persons, living or dead, is purely coincidental.
This book is licensed for your enjoyment only. This book may not be re-sold or given away to other people. If you would like to share this book with another person, please purchase an additional copy for each recipient. If you were reading this book and did not purchase it, or it was not purchased for your use only, then please buy your copy. Thank you for respecting the hard work of this and all authors.

Pitch:
Standing in the blood of the man who tried to kill him, the boy, almost a man, froze, horrified at what he had done. The head, separated from the body, lay face down in the forest undergrowth. Blood flowed from the open neck onto the mat of decaying leaves. There had been no time. There had been no time to think. No time to plan. Only one would walk away from that confrontation in the woods. The boy had gotten the better of this man who had killed many before him.
When the woman, dressed to blend into the forest, emerged from behind the trees to admire his handiwork, pointing her crossbow at him, he thought he might have killed for naught. Little did any of the handful of people standing in the forest that day know the changes that this one death would put in motion.

Chapter 1

The Princess, her maids, and their guardsmen escorts walked to town to buy fabric. As they passed by the butcher's shop, one of the chickens got loose. The butcher's son raced after the frightened squawking bird, but he did not catch it until after it had become entangled in the lace at the hem of the Princess' dress. The boy prostrated himself on the hard ground as he disengaged the unruly chicken.

"My Princess, the chicken has ruined your dress. What do you wish me to do to make this up to you? Please do not be angry with me."

"Rise, boy, there is no harm done. The dirt will wash out."

The boy stood holding the outraged chicken under his arm. The chicken's wing smacked him in the face, and he sputtered, completely embarrassed.

The Princess laughed. She held out her hand for him to kiss.

The boy gently took her hand with the one that was not holding the chicken and bent over to kiss it.

As soon as the boy's lips touched the Princess' gloved hand, one of the guards yelled, "Mind your manners, boy!" and hit him on the back of the head with his whip handle.

The boy spun around, pulled the dagger he kept to ward off thieves, and tossed the chicken at his assailant.

The boy did not know who shouted for him to run, but he suspected it was his father. He heard the whip crack once near his head and bolted for the city gates.

The boy ran as if his life depended on it. He knew that the dagger half the length of his arm he carried in his right hand was no match for the pointed, metal-tipped whip twice the length of his body repeatedly cracking behind him.

He knew these woods well, having spent time here hunting small game. The path he followed ended in a cliff as high as a hundred men. He could jump over the cliff and hope to catch one of the trees that grew out of the sandy face of the cliff, but then, he would only have to face the metal-tipped whip again some other time.

The whip cracked less than a stride-length behind him. He needed a way to rid himself of this threat forever. Spotting a sturdy tree about his thigh's diameter with smooth bark, he reached out with his left hand and hooked it on the tree. His motion carried him around the tree without slowing him down. His feet flew out from underneath him, but his hand and arm held firm as he slid on the smooth bark.

His pursuer was too surprised to stop. The hunter became the hunted. The boy grabbed the man's long, greasy hair with his left hand and, with his right, in a single, smooth, practiced move, drew the dagger across the throat of the man who would have killed him. Not wishing to cause a death that was any more painful than necessary, he finished the job and removed the man's head.

Even a person this evil should not be made to suffer in death. Death should be as swift and as efficient as possible. The boy knew that had he been caught, his death at the hands of this criminal would have been slow and painful. He did not wish such a thing on his worst enemy, who this was.

The boy stood gasping for air as the body followed its head to the ground. He did not know how long he stood there, frozen in fear. The boy knew he could not return to his home, but he had no idea what he should do now. He heard a branch snap in the woods beside him. He turned to look.

A woman wearing clothes that blended into the forest stood with a crossbow pointed at him. The bowstring was tense, the bow ready to send the bolt into his chest. Less than two stride-lengths away, there would be no way to evade the arrow. She was almost as tall as he was, although she was slender and graceful of bearing. She wore her long hair tightly braided in the manner of the noblewomen of the city. Only the noblewomen could afford a servant who could take the time to weave such an intricate arrangement. The braid formed a crown on the top of her head. The noblewomen of the city would adorn the braid with pins mounted with gems. This woman's braid was unadorned.

Clutching the bloody dagger, the boy put his hands in the air and backed up. A noblewoman in the forest with an unadorned braid holding a crossbow pointed at him made no sense. Commoners did not approach noblewomen unless invited, much less ask why they were alone in the woods.

The woman smiled. "Nice piece of work. You have done well."

The boy realized that she was not about to kill him quite yet, but he did not relax. He nodded as he trembled.

"Killing a king's guard is not an easy thing to do. How did you do it?"

The boy hesitated. He was not sure how to answer the question. He bowed, holding his dagger well away from his body. "It's like killing a cow, Milady. You do it as fast as you can, so there is not so much pain."

"When you kill a cow, you stroke the knife from back to front. Do you not?"

"Yes, Milady, I didn't have time to get my arm back around."

The woman pointed to the blood on the boy's smock. "Do you often kill members of the king's guard?"

"No, Milady. I am the son of the butcher. We see a lot of blood."

"That makes sense."

The woman rested the crossbow against a tree and unsheathed her sword. It was a brightly polished long sword with a curved end slightly lighter than a saber. It was intended to keep one's opponent at a distance. She impaled the head on the point and examined it. "Ah, yes, I know this one. He was a particularly nasty piece of work. You have done the city a favor by killing him."

"Yes, Milady. Thank you, Milady."

The woman flung the head over the cliff hard enough that it splashed in the river below. She motioned for the boy to lower his arms.

"Boy, whatever your name was is of no matter. You are a fugitive. From this day forward, you shall be known as Cleaver. You have earned the name because you are the son of a butcher. A cleaver is a butcher's tool, and you cleaved off the man's head in one stroke. You do know you can never go home again."

"Yes, Milady. What shall I call you?"

"Milady."

"Yes, Milady."

"We should dispose of the body."

"Yes, Milady."

They dragged the body to the cliff and pushed it over. Only when it had come to rest at the bottom of the cliff did they turn away.

"Take off your clothes. Leave them in a pile near the cliff."

"My clothes, Milady?"

"Yes, all of them except your boots and underpants, if you wear any. Keep the dagger and the belt. We will need that."

"Yes, Milady."

Cleaver stood in his boots, undershorts, and his leather belt with his dagger. "Milady, why did we do that?"

"Predators will smell the blood. They'll be here soon. No point in asking for trouble. Time to go."

Milady pulled a shirt dyed to match the forest colors from the pack she wore, which held her quiver of arrows. "Here, put this on."

Cleaver donned the long shirt, which fell almost to his knees.

Milady picked up the crossbow, relaxed the bow, and used it to point to a path. They walked silently along the forest paths until they were well away from the place where the fight had been.

"So, young Cleaver, why were you running through the forest with a king's guardsman trying to whip you to death?"

"He said I made an improper advance on the Princess, but I didn't. I swear it."

"The Princess is beautiful. Do you not think of marrying her?"

"No, Milady. She is delicate, like a china doll. Look at me. I would break her. I wouldn't mean to, but I break things. You don't break people if you can help it."

"So, you are afraid that you would hurt her."

"Yes, Milady."

"Is there someone you love?"

"Yes, Milady. She is the daughter of the rancher who sells us our stock. She is sturdy and strong. She is used to living on a farm and doing hard work. We talk every Sunday in church."

"How long have you known her?"

"Since we were babies."

"Well, Cleaver, you are among friends. We are scoundrels, every one of us, but we take care of our own."

"Thank you."

They approached a stream.

"Take off your boots."

Milady took off her boots and hiked up her pants. Cleaver did as he was told.

"Follow me."

They walked in the stream until they came to an old tree partially felled by the running water. Milady parted some of the roots and stepped gingerly under the tree. From there, they found a cave. Part of the cave was natural, but part of it had been dug out by hand. A strong wind from the cave entrance pushed Cleaver forward.

They walked for a while in the darkness, following a rope pinned to the wall at regular intervals. The wind on Cleaver's back was surprisingly cold. Eventually, they came to a large opening in the cave. The cavern was lit by torches mounted around the walls. The wind, which had been at Cleaver's back, shifted so that it passed the flames and went out a large hole in the cavern's roof. As Cleaver looked around, he understood. This was an abandoned copper mine. A score of these littered the countryside. A dozen men stood over a freshly killed buck.

"Ladies and gentlemen, this is Cleaver. He killed Whipsaw."

The people in the room murmured in amazement.

"He is the son of a butcher." Milady turned to Cleaver. "Do you know how to deal with that?" She pointed to the buck."

Cleaver smiled. "Yes, Milady. I won't waste any of it."

"Good. Be quick about it. We have work to do."

"Yes, Milady." Cleaver pulled his dagger and went to address the buck. He shook his head. "In the future, please try to be more careful. This arrow alone was enough to kill this poor animal. Wait until you have a clear shot. As it is, we will have a hard time using this pelt."

One of the men stood and faced Cleaver. "Who are you to tell me how to kill a buck?"

"I am the son of a butcher. I have killed many deer with more skill than this."

"I am a warrior and..."

"Arrow! That is enough." Milady interposed herself between the two. "Cleaver killed Whipsaw with that dagger, and I do not wish to lose my best archer in a brawl. He is right. You are impatient. You take many shots when one would do the job."

"Yes, Milady."

"We have a new mission. Make sure all the archers have double the number of arrows you usually carry. I will need a like number for my crossbow."

"Yes, Milady."

"We are confronting a large force in the morning and will need every arrow to count."

"Yes, Milady."

"Britches!"

"Yes, Milady?"

"Ah, there you are. Cleaver will need a complete set of leathers. He will be on the front line tomorrow."

"Should I leave space in the vest for chain mail, Milady?"

Milady scanned Cleaver as he industriously dressed the buck. "No, the weight will slow him down. He needs to be fast."

"Yes, Milady."

"Thank you, Britches."

"Yes, Milady."

"Shields!"

"Milady, do you think the young man would be better off with a short sword, a broad sword, a saber, or one like yours?"

Shields held out four options for her examination.

"How do you do that?"

"Do what, Milady?" Shields bowed at the waist as he said this.

"Know what I need before I ask for it?"

"I pay attention, Milady. It's not that hard."

"The saber." Milady shook her head slowly as Shields returned to his work area for a sheath.

"Cleaver! How are you with a bow and arrow?"

"Good on a heavy short bow at short range, Milady."

Milady sighed. "Well, that answers that question. Arrow! When we return from this mission, you will train Cleaver on the longbow."

"Yes, Milady."

"Tinker!"

A woman standing over an anvil with a sheet of hammered steel in her hand shouted back, "Milady, do you want an infantry helmet or an archer's helmet?"

"Infantry. We don't know if he can shoot a longbow yet."

"Yes, Milady. Too pretty a face to leave unprotected."

Milady sat at one end of a long table. An elderly man with scars on his face approached her.

"Hello, Cheesy, how are your knees holding out?"

"As well as can be expected, Milady."

"We have herbs for the pain."

"Yes, Milady. I take them at night, so I can sleep. They make me dizzy in the day, and I do not wish to burn myself."

"I am glad you are here. What are we eating today?"

"Rabbit stew, fresh bread, and cheese."

"Thank you."

"Indeed, Milady. It is my honor to serve with you."

"Even when I was little, you always knew the right thing to say."

"I try, Milady."

"Have you been watching Cleaver? Does he know what he is doing?"

"Yes, Milady. He is the most skilled. The next time we go into town, we should get him a proper set of knives. He is doing a good job with the dagger, but he would be better with proper tools."

"Wouldn't buying a complete set of butcher knives alert someone that he is alive?"

"Yes, and that is a good thing. By morning, when Whipsaw does not return, it will be common knowledge that Whipsaw is dead. He was last seen chasing the boy into the forest. Neither has been seen since. Whipsaw always brings his victims' bloody bodies to the city to display them in the town square. The boy would do no such thing. When Whipsaw fails to return, the common assumption would be that both had died. By purchasing the knives, we alert the family that the boy still lives and is with us. The word will spread from there. Your stature and the respect with which you are held will increase."

"Whipsaw was the most hated of the King's guards. If we can get Bludgeon tomorrow, we will have done the city a great service."

"Is Bludgeon the target for tomorrow?"

"Yes, and Bluebeard."

"The bandit?"

"Yes, according to my sources, they intend to ambush the convoy from the copper mine at the river crossing tomorrow. We will be there to see that the convoy gets through safely."

"Do you need me with you?"

"I need you to stay here with Doc, Baker, Stew, Bones, Quack, and Herbs to guard the entrances. Make sure you have enough arrows to hold off a small army."

Cleaver finished with the buck, returned to the stream to clean himself, and came back inside to eat. He was not a fan of rabbit stew, but tonight, it tasted like the best meal he had ever had. He was fitted for his leathers his helmet, and issued his sword. He squeezed in a little sleep before leaving with the others for the morning's mission.

Chapter 2

Fifty men and women left the cave before dawn through a half dozen concealed entrances. The copper mine owner had contracted them to keep the bandits from stealing the convoy's load. They were also to keep the King's guard from extracting additional taxes over what the mine owner had already paid the King directly.

Cleaver's mission was simple. If the King's guard did not find and attack the bandits before the convoy reached the river crossing, he was to leave his hidden position on the call of the grackle. He would then, as silently as possible, sneak up behind the bandits and kill as many of them as he could. The bandits were not as well trained as the King's guards, and many of them were drunk, so killing the bandits would be easier than killing the guards. Bluebeard was to be spared so he could be interrogated before being put to death.

The archers would concentrate on the King's guard. Twenty guardsmen were expected. The ideal situation would be to have the bandits and the King's guard slaughter each other and leave their fighters to mop up and kill whoever remained. All the guardsmen and the bandits were to be killed. The only prisoners were to be Bludgeon and Bluebeard.

Cleaver was not thrilled with the plan. The mass slaughter was not a problem for him. After all, killing is part of a butcher's life. The plan was just too obvious to have any chance of success. Any fool with half a brain could know that the river crossing was the most vulnerable point in the trip. So, if one was expecting an attack, that was where it would happen. The crossing was at a wide spot in the river, which was so open as to make it virtually indefensible. Cleaver had often gone fishing there and had brought home plenty of fish to feed his family and sell to their customers.

To Cleaver's way of thinking, the roads approaching the crossing, which were hemmed in with tall trees on both sides, were a better place to mount an attack. Accordingly, his chosen hiding place was halfway up a large pine tree where he could see the crossing and the roads to it from all directions. He climbed the tree in the last remnants of moonlight. He wedged himself between the trunk and some branches. Without the new leather armor, the position would have been uncomfortable, but it was quite lovely with it.

Cleaver heard before he saw the first of the wagons. Cleaver watched the wagons approach. Something made no sense. The wagons had two oxen per team when they should have had four. The oxen were barely straining with their loads. For a load as heavy as the copper should be, the oxen should have been rebelling with every step. The wagon wheels should have left deep ruts in the sand when they passed over a wet spot in the trail. In Cleaver's opinion, the grooves were too shallow.

Cleaver saw the bandits approach from the opposite side of the river. From the positions he and his people had taken, there was no way to sneak up on them from behind. Attacking them from the front would have been suicide. The way they moved carefully from the cover of one tree to the next, they certainly did not appear drunk or poorly trained.

A random breeze blew back the corner of one of the covers on one of the wagons. Before it was yanked back into place, Cleaver saw archers huddled where the cargo should have been. This was a trap.

Cleaver noticed movement on the ridge opposite the road behind where their archers were hidden. Eighty of the King's guards on horseback mounted the open ridge. Another twenty men rode down the hill to the road behind the convoy as it reached the crossing.

The call to attack was the clattering "ching, ching" noise of the grackle. The only other bird call that Cleaver knew was the call of the crow. "CAW CAW CAW!"

Desperately, he called three times, hoping that the delay would be enough to stop their people from falling into the trap.

Cleaver had just finished the third set of calls when the bandits attacked the convoy. The convoy's archers, hidden behind the high wooden sides of the wagons, decimated the bandits. The river ran red with their blood. Perhaps a quarter of the original force of bandits retreated back into the woods, leaving their fallen behind.

The twenty guardsmen, recognizing the archers' lethality and that no taxes were to be collected from this bunch, raised their hands in salute. They rode across the river in pursuit of the remaining bandits.

Cleaver listened to the sounds of battle from his vantage point in the tree. Half of the wagons with the archers crossed the stream and waited on the other side. Half remained on this side. The convoy's archers returned to the cover of the wagons to wait. The plan, whatever it was, had not been fully revealed. Cleaver noticed motion in a tall pine tree on the opposite side of the road from where he watched the action. Someone was climbing the tree. When the person found a place to sit, they turned to face him. It was Milady. She flashed him a quick "thumbs up" and turned her attention to the river.

The next time Milady looked in his direction, Cleaver pointed at the eighty guardsmen still on the ridge behind her. She glanced over her shoulder and flashed a "thumbs up" sign.

The eighty guardsmen on the ridge waited patiently while the twenty guardsmen in the initial detail chased bandits through the woods and occasionally killed one. Most of Milady's fighters silently held their positions. The archers, taking their lead from Cleaver, climbed high in the surrounding trees. They could see their targets better, and the heavy branches offered them some protection from archers on the ground.

A second convoy, four times the first, rumbled down the road from the mine. These wagons were pulled by teams of four oxen. The oxen strained and resisted with every step. The ruts left in the wet spot were deep and became deeper with every wagon that passed. The convoy reached the soft sand of the crossing. The guardsmen on the ridge held their position. The archers who had waited by the river moved the oxen from the empty wagons to the loaded wagons. The four-oxen teams became six-oxen teams as they struggled across the soft sand of the river bottom.

Once a team of six had pulled the wagon across the river, the teams were separated. Two were brought back across to help with the next wagons. In this manner, by rotating the assisting oxen, the wagons were safely hauled across the river. The wagons the archers had arrived in were abandoned. All the oxen were hitched to wagons as the convoy prepared to depart. Once the convoy was ready and the trail boss seemed satisfied with his convoy's status, he mounted the lead wagon. The guardsmen who had gone after the bandits, some of them covered in blood, blocked the road.

An argument developed, and the guardsman drew his sword on the trail boss. The dispute ended abruptly when an arrow from a crossbow appeared in the guardsman's chest, and he fell from his horse. Before the archers on the ground had a chance to react, five more guardsmen fell to the ground. The trail boss ordered the convoy forward as the convoy's archers attacked the guardsmen. The guardsmen fought bravely, but they were all killed, not, however, without killing six of the convoy's archers.

The wagon train rumbled away, leaving the dead and dying behind.

The eighty guardsmen on the ridge were too far away to lend assistance, but they raced as fast as possible to catch the fleeing convoy. Milady's archers in the trees picked off the wave of guardsmen galloping along the road. Some guardsmen escaped the archers hidden in the trees only to be ambushed by Milady's people on the ground and dragged off their horses. Still, about ten of the remaining, including Bludgeon, raced through the kill zone. Cleaver dropped out of his tree onto one of the liberated horses and pursued Bludgeon. Bludgeon was a frequent visitor to his father's shop, and Cleaver had scores to settle with him.

Tinker, Britches, Shields, and a woman named "Stealth" about his age, who looked like she could be his sister if he had one, charged on stolen steeds behind him.

A crossbow bolt appeared in the rearmost guardsman's back as he crossed the river, knocking him from his horse. Another arrow fell short, and soon Cleaver and his party were out of range of help. The surviving convoy archers killed four of the remaining guardsmen with the loss of two of their own.

The five surviving guardsmen turned to face the threat approaching them from behind. Neither group carried projectile weapons. As long as they stayed out of range of the fleeing convoy's archers, whatever happened here would be hand-to-hand. Bludgeon sat on his horse at the "V" point with his four soldiers behind him. Similarly, Cleaver stood on his horse with Tinker and Britches to his left. Shields and Stealth stood to his right. Cleaver stood with four of his new friends whose training he did not know against five of the King's guardsmen, whose combat proficiency was far too familiar.

They stood in silence, with only the fidgeting of the horses to mark the time.

Bludgeon knit his brows in confusion. "Don't I know you?"

"You might. I certainly know you."

"You're supposed to be dead."

"That would be the rumor. Strange how such rumors get started. That's not how things worked out. You will find your friend's body a thousand stride-lengths downriver. His head may be further downstream. We can arrange for you to join him."

Bludgeon tipped his head. "You killed Whipsaw?"

"I did."

"Did you have help?"

"Not in killing him. I did have help disposing of the body, as I shall have help disposing of yours."

Bludgeon laughed so hard that tears came to his eyes. "I knew this would happen. I knew one of his bastards would get him in the end."

Bludgeon laughed for a bit. Regaining control, he said, "Boy, you killed your father." He laughed so hard that he leaned back in the saddle.

"My father is the butcher."

Bludgeon laughed again. "How old are you, boy?"

"There are conflicting accounts of my age. My mother is no longer with us to settle the differences."

"That's because Whipsaw raped your mother while your father was away at war. He raped a lot of women. Nobody tried to stop him."

"That's not true!" Cleaver shouted.

"Not only that, but the lady to your right is your half-sister. The man to your left is your half-brother. The farm girl you are so fond of is your half-sister, but best of all, the one you call 'Milady' is also your half-sister."

"That's not true!"

Bludgeon spurred his horse with his arm out, intending to knock Cleaver off his horse and escape, but Cleaver drew his dagger quickly enough to plunge it into Bludgeon's side. The blade barely penetrated the leather armor and chain mail underneath, but it did break the skin and draw blood. The impact was enough to knock them both from their horses. The horses fled.

Bludgeon and Cleaver stood in fighting stances, facing each other. Cleaver was larger and, being younger, was faster, but Bludgeon was combat-trained, which Cleaver was not. Cleaver drew the saber he had never used. The dagger was already in his hand. Bludgeon drew a massive double-sided broadsword. Their companions sat on their horses, fascinated by the action in front of them. Not one lifted a finger to help.

Cleaver watched Bludgeon's movements and compared them to the cattle he had wrestled to bring them inside to be slaughtered. Bludgeon's motions were not that different. Hunched over to present as small a target as possible, protected by his helmet, Cleaver waited for Bludgeon's first move. He did not have to wait long. Cleaver sidestepped the lunge, and the broadsword's flat side clanged off the side of the helmet. Cleaver grabbed Bludgeon's sword arm and twisted it around so he was behind Bludgeon's back. Cleaver dropped his sword and put his dagger to Bludgeon's throat. He was about to remove Bludgeon's head when he felt a knife at his throat.

"Don't kill him," Milady ordered. "We need him."

Cleaver looked up to see a half dozen archers with crossbows. One of the crossbows was aimed at him.

"If I release him, he will run."

"No, he won't. Everyone get off your horses."

When everyone was off their horses, Milady ordered, "Release the horses. We cannot care for them. They will find their way home."

Stealth asked, "What do we do with these four?"

Milady stared at them for a moment. "The King lost almost a hundred guardsmen today. We have Bludgeon. Bluebeard is still out there. Someone should clean up these bodies before the animals do. They have families that should know what happened to them. Take their boots, their pants, and their weapons. They can walk home."

"Yes, Milady."

The four soldiers, minus their pants and boots, waded across the river under the watchful eye of a dozen camouflaged denizens of the forest.

"Cleaver, Britches, and Tinker make a stretcher for Bludgeon and tie him to it. Blindfold him. Take him to the treehouse and leave him tied up. We will come back for him in a few days. Shields and Stealth, you are coming with me. We have a copper mine to visit. The rest of you make sure that these four go straight home and do not linger along the way."

Once the stretcher was done and Bludgeon securely attached, Cleaver asked, "Milady, is it true?"

"Is what true?"

"That you are my half-sister?"

"Except for Cheesy, almost all of us share the same father, including those four we just sent packing and the Princess."

"Whipsaw raped the Queen?"

"Yes."

"Were some of the guardsmen we killed related to us?"

"Yes, about a quarter of them."

Bludgeon began to laugh, and Cleaver stuffed the leg of one of his soldier's pants in his mouth.

Cleaver touched the point of his dagger to Bludgeon's throat. "I can still kill you and dress you like a hog."

Chapter 3

"King Orange, might I interrupt you for a bit?"

"Yes, Orange Adviser, what is so urgent that you must interrupt my meal?"

"Sire, news has arrived about the hundred riderless horses that returned to the stables yesterday."

"In what form?"

"Four of the guardsmen who were among the hundred have returned."

"Have they spoken to anyone?"

"Not that I am aware of Your Highness."

"Send them in."

Four filthy men clad only in their jackets and undershorts prostrated themselves on the floor in front of the King.

"Get up, you fools. You can't speak to me from there."

The four stood and pushed one of their comrades forward.

"Your Highness, Sire, Your Majesty, we have sad news to report. Please forgive us, for we have failed you."

"I determined that on my own by your condition. Tell me something I can't observe with my own eyes."

"Your Highness, please forgive us for appearing before you this way. We rode into a trap, Sire. They mowed us down with arrows from the wagons, from the trees, and with soldiers on the ground."

"Who, they?"

"The miner sent wagons full of archers ahead of the main convoy."

"Prudent. Go on."

"When the bandits attacked the decoy, the archers killed most of them."

"Nicely done. Did the archers get Bluebeard?"

"I don't know, Sire."

"Then, what happened?"

"Twenty of our men peacefully rode past the decoy to kill the rest of the bandits."

"Did they succeed?"

"They killed some, but I don't know if they got them all."

"Then what happened?"

"The remainder of the convoy with the copper came to the river, and they pulled the loads across."

"Did no one try to stop them?"

"The leader of the twenty men who had gone after the bandits stopped at the head of the convoy as they were about to depart to demand the additional taxes as you requested, Sire."

"Yes, and then? Out with it, boy."

"He was shot in the chest with a crossbow."

"Where was the crossbow shot from?"

"Across the river in a tree."

"Do you mean to tell me that someone with a crossbow killed one of my guardsmen from a tree thirty or forty stride-lengths away?"

"Not just one, Sire. Four or five guardsmen died like that. There were many arrows, and all twenty of the guardsmen in the advance group were killed. Most were killed by the convoy's archers."

"Where were you while this was going on?"

"Sire, I was with Bludgeon and the main force of eighty men. We were on the high ridge overlooking the river crossing. When the first guardsman died, Bludgeon ordered us to ride after the convoy. They were trying to escape."

"And?"

"It was a bloodbath, Sire. Archers in the trees killed our riders as they came down the road. Foot soldiers came out of the brush to kill more. Bludgeon got through. About ten of us made it across the river."

"Ten out of eighty?"

"Yes, Sire. When we reached the other side of the river, archers from the convoy attacked us, and then it was only Bludgeon and the four of us."

"Five men out of a hundred survived?"

"Yes, Your Majesty. We heard horses behind us, so we turned to face them. They had taken five horses from the dead men. Bludgeon knew their leader. It was the butcher's boy that Whipsaw chased into the woods."

"Are you sure?"

"Yes, Sire. They talked. I recognized him, too. My mother buys meat from their shop. He is the only honest butcher in town, Sire."

"So, the boy is alive, and Whipsaw has not returned."

"Yes, Sire. The boy told Bludgeon that he had killed Whipsaw. He said that Whipsaw's body was a thousand stride-lengths downstream, and his head had washed further downriver."

"So, you mean to tell me that the butcher boy killed Whipsaw, one of my best guardsmen, and beheaded him?"

"Sire, Your Highness, Sire, that is what the boy said. I do not know if any of what was said is true."

"Bludgeon has been known to stretch the truth to shock his enemies. Perhaps the boy did as well."

"Sire, all I know is that Bludgeon tried to sweep the boy off his horse, and the boy stabbed him. The boy knocked them both to the ground."

"How do you know the boy stabbed Bludgeon?"

"I saw fresh blood on his vest, Sire."

"What happened when they were both on the ground?"

"They faced off for a bit until Bludgeon lunged for the boy. The boy sidestepped and got behind Bludgeon. The boy was about to cut off Bludgeon's head when a woman and some archers came upon them from behind. The woman ordered the boy to stop. They wanted Bludgeon as a captive. She told us to get off our horses and sent the horses away. She had us remove our boots, pants, and weapons. She had some of her fighters escort us part of the way home. Here we are, Your Majesty."

King Orange sighed. "Did the woman wear her hair in a braid like a noblewoman?"

"Yes, Sire, she did. She wore clothes that would blend into the forest. The dagger she held to the boy's throat had a jewel-encrusted handle."

King Orange abruptly stood from his place, his face twisted in rage. "Gentlemen, it would not do for the kingdom's citizens to know that a band of renegades killed so many of my best guardsmen. Orange Adviser will take you to my quarters. You will be fed and provisioned. You will leave immediately with a squad to recover the bodies of the fallen. We will notify the families. You will search to determine if Bluebeard is among the dead. You will return with your report."

The men bowed. "Thank you, Your Majesty."

King Orange opened a door. "Up the stairs, first door on the left."

Once the men had scampered out of sight, Orange Adviser turned to King Orange. "Sire, what will you do with Whipsaw dead?"

King Orange scratched his eyebrow. "I will need to hire a new rapist. Having my brother do it was convenient. He was so good at it. He was brilliant. What better way is there to control a man than if he knows that he can't protect his wife from the King's personal sexual predator?"

"Yes, Sire, you could do it yourself."

"The thought of putting any part of my pristine anatomy inside one of those dirty, smelly things turns my blood cold. Why do you think

I had Whipsaw impregnate the Queen? No. I will find someone else. You're too old for the job. The first husband you ran into would kill you, and I need you here."

"Yes, Your Majesty. What about Bludgeon, Sire? Would he be a good choice?"

"The woman of the woods will kill him. Even if she spares his life, he will be of no use to me when she finishes with him, and I will have to kill him."

"Yes, Your Majesty."

"Collect a dozen of your most loyal men. Take these four back into the woods. I am not interested in the bodies. Collect the uniforms and weapons. See to it that these four never return."

"Yes, Your Majesty, with pleasure, Your Majesty."

"I don't care how you feel about it, just do it."

Chapter 4

Milady, Shields, and Stealth returned well after dark. Cheesy greeted them as they sat to eat. "How did it go with the miners?"

"Not well. The mine is abandoned. The tunnel is collapsed two stride lengths inside. They even took the metal from the roofs of the buildings." Milady put her head down into her hands.

"How did we not know this was happening?" Cheesy asked.

"I would ask Copper-top since she was our resident spy, but she's missing. We didn't find her body, so she must have made a deal with them."

"So, now, what do we do?"

"The King will send his men to collect what he can from the guardsmen we killed. We need to go back and retrieve the weapons and whatever uniforms that don't have so much damage that we can't reuse them."

"Already done, Milady. The uniforms are soaking in the pool in the north excavation. The weapons, boots, and belts are high and dry in the west excavation."

"Had they all died when you arrived?"

"They were all dead when we left, Milady."

Milady paused. She could not reprimand her only remaining family friend. He knew how she felt about such things. "Has Cleaver returned?"

"He is in the east pond washing the blood from his body."

"I will eat later."

"As you wish, Milady."

The east pond was a wide spot in one of the streams that ran through the underground labyrinth of mine shafts and caves. Almost a man-height deep at its deepest point, it was four stride lengths wide and ten stride lengths long. The fresh water flowed slowly enough to be comfortable but quickly enough to carry the soap and dirt out to some Artesian well far away. It was the most likely place to find the people who lived in these caverns after a battle.

Cleaver was exiting the water when Milady approached. His butcher's smock and his combat leathers had hidden the features of his body. As he stood dripping at the edge of the water in his nakedness, all Milady could do was gasp. The musculature of his chest would make any woman swoon. The soft shadow on his face held the promise of a full and dark beard. Tinker sat on a rock, similarly appreciating the view as Milady approached. Milady hissed at Tinker, "He is your brother."

Tinker grinned. "More's the pity. He's yours, too."

Milady shook her head. "I guess being the butcher's kid does have its advantages."

Tinker chuckled. "I guess. You should ask him to wash your back. He's surprisingly gentle."

That was the first that Milady noticed that Tinker's hair was still wet. "Did you?"

Tinker giggled. "No. He's my brother. I have two brothers at home. I know the rules."

Milady stared at Cleaver as he grabbed a cloth to wipe himself dry. He had not noticed Milady and Tinker staring at him due to the uneven lighting from the wall-mounted torches. After he had wrapped the cloth around himself, Milady called to him. "Cleaver, did you have any trouble with the prisoner?"

"No, Milady. We left him tied naked on the floor. The water drop from the break in the rock dripped where it would fall into his mouth if he opened his mouth. He will not die of thirst."

"Very good. The prisoner can stay there for a day or two. I will send you to get him when it is time. You have to promise not to kill him."

"Yes, Milady. But that will be a hard promise to keep."

"I understand. I have a mission for you. Before dawn, you, Arrow, Stealth, Shields, Blade, and Dragon will return to the site of the battle. We expect that the King's guardsmen will return to collect the uniforms and weapons we have already collected. Hide in the trees. Wait until they are finished. Then you will separate the four we freed yesterday and bring them to the lodge-house. As soon as they are away from the others, you will kill all but the wagon drivers."

"Why are we taking those four?"

"We need to know how much King Orange knows about us. They will be able to tell us."

"Yes. Milady. Milady? Might I ask a question?"

"Certainly. I reserve the right to not answer."

"Of course, Milady. How did you know to meet me in the woods?"

"Watcher saw you run out of the city gate with Whipsaw on your tail and alerted a nearby patrol. We had a plan for the next time Whipsaw left the city. This was not the first time he had chased someone he intended to execute out of the city gates. This was the first time he failed. The patrol warned me, and we tracked you. I was looking forward to killing Whipsaw, but I can't say I was disappointed that you did it."

"Thank you, Milady."

"Welcome home."

✕

KING ORANGE STOOD TO greet a guardsman captain. The captain saluted.

"Did you extract the punishment from the miners?"

"No, your Majesty. The mine was collapsed. They were gone. They took everything. They took the metal from the buildings and dumped slag in the wells."

"They must have left something."

"No, Your Highness. They knocked down the chimneys. The smelters were gone. We didn't find any fresh graves. Everything was cold. All the food stores had been emptied. Even the cooking utensils were gone."

"How long do you think they had been planning this?"

"Must have been months, Sire."

"Where do you think they went?"

"Sire, the nearest mineral deposits worth mining are a four-day ride on a fast horse."

"Right in the middle of that barren desert, we fought so hard to win in the last war."

"Yes, Your Majesty."

"We lost legions of good men fighting for that worthless desert. Take two men. Find the convoy and report back to me."

"Yes, Your Majesty."

CLEAVER MET HIS PARTY in the main room, where they would eat before heading out. He knew Arrow, Stealth, and Shields from the previous mission. As they took their places, Cleaver greeted them as the family they were. Blade and Dragon were new. A young man sat opposite him. Cleaver studied him for a few seconds. "I know you. We called you 'Dragon Breath' in school. You must be the 'Dragon,' Milady mentioned."

The newcomer stood and bowed. "One and the very same. It is my honor to be serving with you, my humble friend, Cleaver."

Cleaver laughed. "Humility was never my strength. You must be thinking of someone else."

"I knew when I saw you running through the woods with Whipsaw on your tail that you would land here. Look, the rules say we're supposed to leave our past behind when we come here, but the way you dressed that buck and the way you took off Whipsaw's head, I'm glad you didn't."

"You saw that?" Cleaver asked.

"I did. I thought you were a goner there for a bit, but then you spun around the tree. It was all I could do to keep from cheering for you."

Stealth agreed, "That was amazing. I almost couldn't believe what I was seeing."

Dragon said, "And then you took off his head with no more emotion than if he was a cow or a pig. One slice and done. Awesome."

"Thank you."

Dragon stared earnestly at Cleaver. "You were always the smartest kid in school. We need that here. But I also know that you let your anger carry you away. We've lost too many good people to their anger. Please, we know what you can do because of what you did yesterday. Think with your head."

"I will."

The last member of the group took a seat as Dragon was speaking. "Dragon's right. Think with your head, but trust your instincts. It's too easy to get killed around here."

Cleaver scanned the array of knives attached to the newcomer's vest and said, "You must be 'Blade' I was told to expect."

"I doubt that you remember me from school, but I remember you. Dragon doesn't like to admit it, but he's smarter than most of us. That's why Milady almost always takes him and one other person when she goes out. Sometimes I go. Sometimes Stealth goes, and Arrow may join us."

"Are those knives as deadly as they look?"

Blade removed one of the knives from her vest and handed it to Cleaver. It was light in his hand.

"I can kill a man at ten strides with that," she said.

Cleaver handed the knife back and raised his right hand. "I promise that you will always be my best friend."

Blade laughed. "Dragon will fight for that honor, but I am happy to share."

Blade and Dragon shook hands.

They finished eating, gathered their weapons, and left.

CLEAVER AND HIS TEAM had barely settled into their positions when the guardsman captain and his two men trotted across the river crossing with their pack horses. They were in too much of a hurry for them to be the people Cleaver and his group were waiting for, so they let the group pass unchallenged.

The riders' dust had barely settled when Orange Adviser arrived with his battle group and six wagons. Each wagon had two drivers. They discovered over a hundred naked bodies strewn around the landscape. All the clothes, including the undergarments, had been taken. The uniforms and the weapons they sought were gone.

From their positions in the trees, Cleaver and his team heard Orange Adviser scream and rave. Cleaver did not remember the last time he had heard anyone so angry. Of course, he also never witnessed the kind of carnage he saw below him. While the guardsmen remained on their horses and watched, Orange Adviser ordered the wagon drivers to load up the bodies. The guardsmen fanned out in the woods, looking for threats. Ground pounders that they were, they did not think to look up to see the danger waiting in the branches for them to finish with the bodies.

The four guardsmen who had survived the previous battle requested Orange Adviser's permission to cross the river. They wished to search to determine if Bluebeard had been killed, survived, or if he had been there at all. Distracted by his fury, Orange Adviser let them go. They crossed the river slowly and carefully, mindful of the hazards of the river's soft bottom. Cleaver watched them go and knew that one small part of today's mission just got easier.

Blade had chosen the same tree as Cleaver, and they sat back to back with their backs against the trunk between them.

"Hey, Blade," Cleaver whispered. "Do you think we can kill Orange Adviser without getting blood on his clothes?"

"Not the way you do it. You get blood everywhere. Why?"

"Blood is hard to remove from that gold braid. Cheesy is about the same height and build as Orange Adviser. If anyone can impersonate Orange Adviser, it's Cheesy."

"Are you nuts?" Blade whispered in horror.

"It's unfamiliar territory for me, but we do need to think about the possibilities."

"It's completely crazy."

"So, what's your point? Can we do it?"

"We'd have to get him off his horse and kill all the other guardsmen first."

"Agreed."

"Can we think about this a bit?"

The four guardsmen who had crossed the river had gone out of sight. No sounds could be heard past the sound of the water moving over the pebbled river bed. The wagon drivers had picked up the bodies on this side of the river and debated whether to cross. The lead wagon driver instructed his men to turn around so they could return to the city. They could come back for the rest later.

Orange Adviser flew off his horse, drawing his sword as he hit the ground.

Cleaver put his hand in the air and rotated it. The rest of his team could see him from his position. From his shoulder, he pointed to the guardsmen forming up between them and Orange Adviser. He flexed his elbow and pointed again. A volley of arrows sped out of the trees knocking three of the guardsmen from their horses. Not all of the arrows found their marks, but the second volley continued the slaughter. When the first guardsman fell, the wagon drivers panicked and drove their teams as fast as they could away from the arrows falling from the sky that they could not see until the arrow hit something.

Five volleys of arrows killed most, but not all of the guardsmen. The remainder were wounded, some critically. Left alone, they would die without treatment. Only one guardsman remained on his feet, but he was bleeding from two wounds. These were the veterans. These were the men who had accompanied King Orange on the last war. Orange Adviser alone stood unscathed. His soldiers lay dead and dying around him. Once Cleaver and his team were on the ground, recognizing that the lone standing guardsman was the most significant threat, Blade threw one of her knives at the man. The blade penetrated his leather armor and drew blood but did not stop him from advancing on her.

Cleaver raced around the man. The guardsman was so focused on the threat facing him that he did not see Cleaver coming. With a single motion, Cleaver cut the man's throat and removed his head. He threw the head at Orange Adviser, who quivered in his boots. Cleaver recognized that the most merciful thing he could do for the wounded guardsmen on the ground, crying out in pain, was to quickly end their misery. Cleaver moved from one to the next, silently slitting their throats.

Orange Adviser vomited. Fear had forced him to empty his bladder and his bowels.

When Cleaver had finished sending the last of the guardsmen to their eternal rest, he held his bloody dagger menacingly as he approached Blade. "You're good. I'm bad."

Blade glanced at the bodies Cleaver had efficiently and dispassionately dispatched. "I see that. Got it."

The rest of the squad blocked whatever attempt Orange Adviser might have made to escape. Cleaver and Blade advanced on the quivering and crying blob that had been King Orange's most trusted servant until a few heartbeats ago.

"I think we should kill him," Cleaver said. "I want his jacket first."

"I think we should capture him. He may have valuable information."

"We'll take his jacket, so we don't get blood on it when I kill him."

"You can have the stupid jacket, but we're not killing him," Blade shouted.

Blade held Orange Adviser at knifepoint while Cleaver unbuttoned the jacket.

"Look at his shirt. It is so frilly," Cleaver sneered. "Isn't it pretty? Take it off!"

Orange Adviser unbuttoned his shirt and pulled it out of his belt. A dark spot showed at the hem in the back.

Cleaver made gagging noises. "That's nasty! Put it in the river."

Cleaver forced Orange Adviser to remove his boots and clothes to rinse the most offensive pieces in the river.

They bound Orange Adviser, still naked, to a makeshift stretcher and prepared to carry him off. As they were about to leave, they heard a two-fingered whistle from across the river. The four guardsmen from the other day sat on their horses and waved to them. Cleaver waved back. The guardsmen saluted and turned their horses around into the forest.

As the four horsemen left, Cleaver said, "I don't think Milady will be happy that we left that bit unresolved."

Chapter 5

A lieutenant of the guard stood before King Orange. "Your Majesty, Sire, Orange Adviser is missing. His horse has returned. The horses of the twelve guardsmen Orange Adviser took with him have returned riderless. The wagon drivers unloaded the bodies left by the river into the castle courtyard and returned for more. The four guardsmen who came back in their undergarments the other day have not returned, and neither have their horses."

King Orange cursed. "How could a band of bastard renegades led by a woman do this much damage in three days? It all started with the butcher's son. I should see to the butcher."

"With all due respect, Sire, the boy must already know that the butcher is not his father. All you will accomplish is to deny the castle and the guard access to the only honest butcher in town. The butcher is not the problem. He is neither an ally nor an enemy. He is simply a butcher."

"Please send Chronicle Gray."

"Yes, Your Majesty."

Chronicle Gray bowed deeply. "Your Majesty, how might I be of service?"

"With my brother gone, there is no clear line of succession to the throne. Any of his bastard children could claim the throne."

"Yes, Sire, but you will be dead, Sire. How is that of concern?"

"There is a rebellion being organized in the mountains around the old copper mines. They have recently been aggressive and successful.

They have killed more of my men in the last three days than I have lost in any year since the great war."

"I still fail to see how this is of concern."

"If I am overthrown, I need a successor who will look legitimate but will keep me from being put to death."

"I see. Is that person not the Princess? Is she not your legitimate daughter?"

"No, Whipsaw is her father."

"Oh, dear. That does complicate things."

"So, I need to know who the eldest of Whipsaw's bastards are so I can start with the eldest and kill them one at a time until I find one that will support me."

"Well, then, Sire, I do know who the eldest is because Whipsaw bragged about it after the baby was born. She was the daughter of a noblewoman. She disappeared five years ago with her manservant."

King Orange screamed and lifted his fists into the air. "She's leading the insurrection!"

"Then you do have a problem, Sire. Whipsaw told every woman he raped after that about raping the noblewoman. If she was not safe from him, then neither were they."

"Do all the women he raped know this?"

"I suspect that they do. I did not know about the Queen. Since Whipsaw was such a braggart, I suspect that all the women after her knew about that as well."

"You are dismissed."

Chronicle Gray bowed and silently left the room.

THE WAGON DRIVERS RETURNED for their second load of bodies. The twelve guardsmen that had accompanied them on their first trip had been divested of their clothes and weapons. Twenty dead bandits were found on the opposite side of the river. They had been liberated of their weapons, but not their clothes. Bluebeard was not among the bodies. A few more bodies were found where the river had carried them downstream. These few still had their clothes and their weapons.

Whipsaw's headless body was recovered, but his head was not found. It lay in the city plaza unclaimed long after the other corpses had been removed. When the last of the fallen had been identified, and the families had been notified, only Bludgeon and Orange Adviser remained missing.

There was no open celebration of Whipsaw's death. The news that Whipsaw had been beheaded, presumably by the butcher's boy, lifted most citizens' spirits, but not all.

CLEAVER SAT IN THE east pond, gently washing Milady's back.

She sighed. "This is not how I envisioned any of this. It is happening too quickly. I know you did not plan this, but your arrival has upended everything. We're not ready to meet King Orange's guardsmen in open battle."

"Milady, with all due respect, the people have suffered enough. We need to act, but you are right. We can't destroy everything without replacing it with something that works."

"What do you suggest?"

"First, we need to get the farms working again. Farmers are refusing to plant all of their property because of the taxes."

"And how do you suggest doing that?"

"At planting time and at harvest, we put everyone who can work into the fields. The guardsmen, everybody. Even the adults that can't walk can drive a team of horses to pull a wagon."

"And that also means keeping taxes down."

"Yes, we wouldn't need such a large force of guardsmen if we ruled by respect instead of fear."

"We can't face the guardsmen in open battle."

"We don't need to face all the guardsmen. We only need to depose King Orange and pass the leadership to the next in line."

"Whipsaw was King Orange's brother. King Orange has no children of his own. The crown passes to the eldest descendant. That is not the Princess. That is me."

"Oh."

"MILADY, THERE IS A campfire on the other side of the river."

"A campfire?"

"Yes, it is visible from the ridge. It is out in the open on the sand next to a bend in the river."

Milady pondered the news for a moment. "They are either stupid, or they want to be found."

"Or both."

Milady laughed. "That could be true, too. Do we know how many there are?"

"Scout reports that she thinks it's four men and four horses, but she's not sure."

"Well, let's give this one to Cleaver and his group. They work well together."

"Yes, Milady. Do you have specific instructions?"

"Cleaver and Blade will figure out what to do. They did a great job with Orange Adviser."

"As you wish, Milady."

"I guess I should go deal with Bludgeon and Orange Adviser. Have Brute, Strange, and Breaker meet me at the dining hall."

"Yes. Milady."

CLEAVER AND BLADE WALKED out of the woods to find the four missing guardsmen sitting around the campfire. They were roasting a rabbit on a spit. They had stew in a pot and some aromatic herbal concoction in another pan. Two more rabbits hung nearby.

The four men were relaxed and appeared to be drinking whatever the herbal thing was. The one turning the spit said, "Greetings. The rabbit is almost done. Would you like some?"

Cleaver sighed. "If you gentlemen intend to survive in the wild, you need to learn the right way to dress a rabbit. Would you like me to show you?"

One of the other men said, "It's the butcher's son. Yes! Yes, please show us how to dress a rabbit."

Blade glanced at Cleaver. "Is he drunk?"

"No, but it's like being drunk. It's the herbs."

Cleaver took down one of the rabbits and carefully explained each step to properly prepare a rabbit for cooking.

They took the first rabbit off the spit and mounted the second one.

"Have you come to kill us?"

"We were told to find you. We were not told what to do after that."

"We would really appreciate it if you didn't kill us. We don't have any right to ask this and will understand if you have to kill us, but we'd rather live."

Cleaver waved his arm for the rest of his group to come out of the woods. He pointed to the pot with the herbal mixture and said, "Don't drink that."

Arrow sat and asked, "Has anyone else been around?"

"Bluebeard stopped by this morning. We had a nice chat. He tried to recruit us, but we chickened out. We gave him bandages and medicine for his wounds from our field packs, and he left. He said to tell the son of the butcher that he respects you, but he does not fear you."

"Not someone we can convert to an ally," Dragon observed.

Cleaver chuckled, "No, but neither will he go out of his way to attack us. It's almost a truce."

One of the guardsmen asked, "What do you want to do about us? We want to go with you."

Cleaver thought about this as he watched the rabbit rotate on the spit. "I don't know if I can trust you. You are still guardsmen."

"Orange Adviser was going to kill us. We can't go back to town any more than you can."

Stealth said, "He does have a point. They can't go back to town. They can't stay here. We can put them in the south dig site. It has a fenced pasture for their horses. The old storage shed is big enough for the four of them, and it's dry."

Cleaver said, "Then if everyone agrees, we should move before we are discovered by anyone we do not wish to see."

The guardsmen were installed in their new home. While they were traveling, they stumbled upon a feral hog. Arrow felled it with two shots. Had he not killed the boar, it would have tried to kill them. When they finally arrived at the south dig site, it was the middle of the night. Stealth and Blade were sent on ahead to deliver the report. Cleaver gave a demonstration of the proper method to dress a hog and left detailed cooking instructions. The four refugees would have food for at least a week.

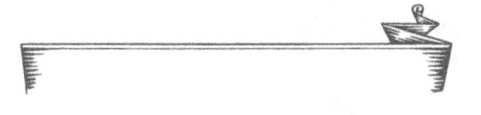

Chapter 6

Milady returned to the cavern covered in blood. She spotted Cleaver eating dinner with Blade.

"You two, come with me."

They strode to the east pond. Milady motioned for them to disrobe, and they settled into the water.

"I should trust your instincts," Milady said once the worst of the blood was off her body.

"In what sense?" Blade asked.

"I should have let you kill both of those monsters on the battlefield."

"That is not your style, Milady," Cleaver said. "It wasn't mine until a few days ago. We can't just run around killing everyone we disagree with as much as we might like to."

Blade commented, "For a guy, you make way too much sense."

"The man who raised me as his son trained to be a clergyman before taking over his father's business when his older brother was killed by a bull."

"Were you his only son?" Blade asked.

"His only child."

"He must miss you." Blade said.

"I suspect that he does. He will bring my cousin into the business, and he will carry on."

"Is your cousin as big and as strong as you?"

"He's younger, but he's bigger and stronger than I was at that age. He's also much kinder and more even-tempered."

Blade laughed. "I would never have called you even-tempered."

"I agree, but whatever I've got going on appears to be working for me now."

Milady said, "Enough of this chatter. I have two bodies to deal with, and we lost Breaker."

"Breaker? Milady?" Blade asked in shock. "He was indestructible."

Cleaver shook his head. "Nobody is indestructible. What happened?"

"I'm not sure. We were getting nothing. I was frustrated. It happened so fast. Bludgeon killed Breaker with his bare hands. Brute and Strange killed Bludgeon. In the confusion, Orange Adviser got loose, and Strange knifed him in the back. Brute was so angry he took off Orange Adviser's head just like you took off Whipsaw's. I've never seen him do that before."

"Was Brute with you that day you followed me into the forest?"

"No, he wouldn't have been able to keep up."

Cleaver paused. "Does Bludgeon still have his head attached?"

"No, why?"

"Stay with me here. I saw a Captain and two men ride out in the direction of the copper convoy. They will be back. When they come back across the river, we intercept them. We don't kill them. We ambush them and take their clothes and weapons. Then we mount Bludgeon's and Adviser's bodies on the pack horses. We make the guardsmen carry the heads and send them to see the King. The spectacle at the gate will distract the city and the guard. We send a task force into the castle through the kitchen loading door and kidnap the Queen and the Princess. The Princess spends most of every day in the kitchen. She loves to cook. King Orange allows this because it keeps her from whining at him all day. After all, she's bored."

"How do you know this?" Milady asked.

"I'm the butcher's son. I made the deliveries."

"Where would we find the Queen?" Blade asked.

"Most likely in the garden growing herbs and spices."

"Are they not guarded?" Milady asked.

"The gardener was a guardsman until he lost his leg below the knee."

"The kitchen?"

"Two guards at the drawbridge, two archers in the towers flanking the drawbridge, two guards at the kitchen door, and two archers on the parapet in the walkway above the kitchen door."

"And you expect a distraction at the city gate will make them abandon their posts?" Blade challenged.

"Of course not. The distraction will only allow our archers to kill the four guardsmen on the ground."

"So, what do we do about their archers?" Blade asked.

Cleaver pursed his lips and thought for a moment. "Did the miners leave behind any of the roofing metal?"

"Yes, a little. Why?"

"We can use it to make shields, big shields."

"Oh, and you expect us to just walk into the castle and then just wander back out?" Milady said in disbelief.

"Yes, in the uniforms of the guardsmen that we killed the other day."

Milady and Blade stared at Cleaver, astounded at the audacity of the plan.

"So, once we have the Queen and the Princess, what do we do with them?" Milady asked.

"We establish them as the new rulers of a matriarchal society replacing the patriarchal society we have now."

"She does not have royal lineage," Blade objected.

"Actually, if we follow a matriarchal line of succession, she has more right to the throne than he does," Milady suggested.

Blade returned her gaze to Cleaver. "You're a guy. Why would you do this?"

"Too many of my friends have died in needless wars of conquest. This nonsense must stop."

"And you think a matriarchal society will be less likely to go to war?"

"I do. A matriarchal society will maintain strong defenses against aggression, but will not themselves be the aggressors."

Blade said, "You went to the same school I did. Where did you learn all this?"

"My grandmother on my mother's side."

Blade and Cleaver brought Milady up to date on their encounter with the four former guardsmen they had parked in the shed.

"Are you certain they were not a threat?"

"They could barely walk, Milady," Blade replied. "Until they stop drinking that herb mixture, they're no good or threat to anyone."

"I'll send Deacon to chat with them. He'll find out if we can trust them."

Blade asked, "Has Deacon recovered from his injuries?"

"Not completely, but I'll send Doc and Bones with him."

Milady sank under the water for a moment. When she came up, she asked, "Do we have any idea when that captain and his men might return?"

"No, idea Milady. We do not know their mission."

"I'll have Cattleman and Roper wait for them along the path. Stealth and Dragon will work with them, and Scout can cross the river to give us warning of their approach."

"What would you like us to do?"

"We'll be walking in the castle's back door. Let's plan it thoroughly."

Chapter 7

"Chronicle Gray, have you news of Bludgeon?"

"Nothing, Your Majesty. We have not heard from him in four days."

"What about Orange Adviser?"

"Nothing, Your Majesty. We have not heard from him in three days."

"What about those four guardsmen that went missing?"

"Nothing, Your Majesty. We have not heard from them in three days."

"What about the captain and his two men?"

"Nothing, Your Majesty. We have not heard from them in three days."

"Bluebeard?"

"Your Majesty, we are not certain that he was at the attack on the convoy. We have no idea where he might be."

"Have the patrols seen anything?"

"Nothing out of the ordinary, Your Majesty."

"Double all the guards. It's too quiet."

"Yes, Your Majesty."

WATCHER REPORTED THAT the castle guard had been doubled, and the attack plan was adjusted. All activity except for preparation for the assault stopped.

Deacon reported that the four wayward guardsmen were harmless, but Cleaver had one more test for them.

Bones reported that the bodies of Bludgeon and Orange Adviser were decomposing. Even though he kept them as cold as the water in the caverns would let him, soon they would be of no use.

SCOUT SPOTTED THE THREE riders as they came through the pass beyond the river's bend shortly after dawn. They could be expected to arrive at the crossing in a quarter-day.

Cleaver had no idea why he thought the riders would avoid the river crossing where the convoy had been ambushed. They could attempt to cross at one of two other two places. While the river could be crossed there, it was deeper, and the water flowed faster. Cleaver placed two of the wayward guardsmen at each of these places to sound the alarm if the riders passed that way.

As soon as Scout flashed the message that the riders were in sight, the assault force left the caverns through multiple concealed entrances.

The captain and the returning guardsmen chose one of the secondary crossing points to ford the river. Two seemingly drunk and disheveled lost guardsmen met the Captain as he reached the bank exiting the river.

"Captain, My Captain, we are so lost. Can you help us find the way home?"

They shouted their opening line as loudly as they could. Dragon heard the call and adjusted the plan.

"You are a disgrace to the uniform. What happened to you?"

"Captain, My Captain, we were chasing bandits, and we got separated from our unit. We were lost in the woods for a night or three. We lost our horses. We were hungry. We ate some of this nice-smelling flower. It has a spicy taste. Would you like some?"

"Back away from me. You stink. Have you no manners?"

"Manners, sir? We were chasing bandits, and we got lost. Bandits have no manners, sir. We were chasing bandits, sir. We got lost, sir."

The wayward guardsman gently rested his hand on the horse's reins. "I told you to back away. You stink."

"I only want to lean on your horse, so I don't fall down. He's a nice horse, so calm and all. You have a nice horse. Does he get out much?"

Two calf-roping ropes materialized out of the trees, looped around the Captain's men, and pulled them to the ground. The remaining wayward guardsmen grabbed the suddenly riderless horses' reins and kept the horses from running away. Dragon and Stealth pointed their crossbows at the captain and ordered him off his horse.

The captain and his men were liberated of their clothes and their weapons. Bludgeon and Orange Adviser's headless bodies were tied to the pack horses upright so that they could be recognized. Decomposition had progressed, and the bodies stank. The captain was lashed to his saddle. The two guardsmen were bound to their horses, which were tethered to the captain's horse. The heads that belonged to the bodies on the pack horses were strapped to their arms. The captain and his men were led to the top of the last hill before they could be seen by the castle's sentries. Dragon and Stealth were the last to fade away into the woods. The captain and his men plodded down the road to the city gate, knowing that crossbows were pointed at their backs.

"WHAT IS ALL THAT NOISE?" King Orange shouted.

"Your Majesty, the captain you sent after the convoy has returned with his men. Bludgeon and Orange Adviser are with them," Chronicle Gray reported.

"Send them right in," King Orange shouted. "It's about time they showed up."

"With all due respect, Your Highness, that will not be possible." Chronicle Gray bowed and trembled.

"What are you talking about? Do you deny me?"

"Sire, Your Highness, Your Majesty, you should see for yourself. Oh, and you should take a squad of guardsmen."

Chronicle Gray bowed even lower as he said, "Sire, I fear your anger if I relate this to you. It would be better if you saw it with your own eyes."

King Orange stormed out of the throne room. He gathered a squad of guardsmen on the way and strode across the drawbridge in front of the castle. As soon as King Orange appeared at the castle gate, the townspeople who had followed the captain, his men, and their macabre cargo fled. The streets and alleys that fronted the castle emptied quickly. Chronicle Gray was too afraid of King Orange's reaction to wish to be anywhere near the front gate, so he retreated to his quarters. Even the squad of guardsmen who King Orange had assembled held back and did not cross the drawbridge. King Orange stood alone and faced the captain.

Only when King Orange stood close enough to be assaulted by the stench of the decomposing bodies did he notice that the captain and his men had cloths binding their mouths shut. The captain was strapped to his saddle. The horse's reins were fastened around his neck. King Orange slowly walked around the three men and five horses carrying the two corpses. Only the swishing of the horses' tails testified that the men and horses were not statues. The townspeople had fled, and even the windows looking out on the square were vacant. A small puff of wind blew the stench toward the castle.

King Orange marched back to the castle and accosted the most senior guards cowering in the doorway. "Untie them. Dispose of the bodies. Get them cleaned up and sent to me."

"Yes, Your Highness."

THE GUARDS STATIONED over the kitchen parapet abandoned their posts as soon as the captain and his gruesome group entered the city. While that saved them from being killed by Arrow or one of his archers, they would likely face a reckoning later. The guardsmen on the ground were taken by surprise. Those who were not killed by the archers were quickly dispatched by Cleaver, Blade, Dragon, and Stealth. The archers in the towers did get some arrows off, but Arrow's archers, having fewer targets and more practice than the tower archers, hit them through the towers' little windows and efficiently ended that portion of the defense.

Cleaver, Blade, Dragon, and Stealth headed for the kitchen with their weapons drawn.

Milady, Cheesy, Brute, Strange, Shields, Stretch, Pug, and Tinker headed for the garden.

The clatter of pots and pans hid whatever noise Cleaver and his crew made as they wended their way through the corridors that led to the kitchen. When they arrived, they found the Princess and four female cooks preparing the midday meal. The Princess was up to her elbows in pastry flour.

The cooks put their hands in the air. They backed away from the tables and stoves where they had been working. Cleaver nodded to them and motioned for them to put their hands down. He sheathed his dagger. He bowed to the Princess and said, "Princess, you must come with me."

"Why? Who are you?"

Cleaver removed the cowl covering his face.

"You? I thought you were dead. You're the..."

Cleaver gently touched his finger to her lips. "Please, Princess, we do not have much time. Guardsmen will be here soon."

"I was so afraid for you." She wrapped her flour-covered arms around him. "You were such a good friend."

"Princess, I am your brother. We must go."

The cooks gasped. Cleaver pointed at them. "You did not hear that."

Cleaver turned back to the Princess. "I am about to throw you over my shoulder and carry you away. The cooks will say that I silently ran in with my companions. I threw you over my shoulder and carried you away while my friends threatened them with knives. You passed out from shock."

Cleaver gently picked the Princess up and settled her over his shoulder. He ran down the corridor with Dragon in front and the rest of his team behind him. They met one guardsman as they ran. Dragon wounded but did not kill him. His testimony would be needed that the Princess was unharmed.

By the time Cleaver reached the drawbridge, the castle guard had realized that something was amiss at the kitchen entrance. Cleaver raced out of the castle protected by the sheets of metal held by the larger of his fellow renegades, which deflected most of the arrows sent in their direction.

When Cleaver reached the horses borrowed from the wayward guardsmen, he realized that he was the first to arrive. The squad taking the Queen must have run into trouble. He placed the Princess in front of him on the horse and rode as fast as possible for the south dig site. They would wait there for further instructions. Blade, Dragon, and Stealth doubled back to assist their comrades in extricating the Queen.

WHEN CLEAVER ARRIVED at the south dig site, the four wayward guardsmen were in front of the small building grooming their remaining horses. They were wearing their uniform britches, but not their shirts. They immediately recognized the Princess and ran to assist her from the horse. They bowed respectfully.

"Princess, welcome to our humble home. It is not what you are used to, but it is dry. The stew has real meat in it. We killed a hog the other day, and it is mighty tasty in the stew. We found some roots and leafy vegetables in the forest. The fruit isn't ripe, but the berries are good. We have some herbal tea if you would like it. It's good for pain."

Cleaver interrupted. He motioned with his hand and shook his head. "Princess, don't drink the tea."

Princess looked up at Cleaver in surprise. "Why not?"

"Princess, you need to keep your wits about you. We don't know how King Orange will react. If he sends Guardsmen after you, we need to move quickly."

Princess paused and looked around. "Why did you tell me that you were my brother? The cooks seemed to know more than they were saying."

Cleaver gently led Princess to a log that was being used as a bench. "When King Orange took most of the men out of the Kingdom to fight the great war, he left Whipsaw in charge. Whipsaw was King Orange's brother. In the three years that the men were gone, Whipsaw raped every woman in the kingdom, including your mother, multiple times. Sometimes two or three in a single day. In the years since he has probably fathered a third of the children born in this kingdom. I believe that these gentlemen before you are also your brothers."

"I find that hard to believe."

"I did, as well. I would not have believed it had I not heard it first from Bludgeon while we were trying to kill each other. He almost succeeded. He thought it was funny that I had killed my father without knowing it. Then I heard it again from Milady."

Princess paused. "I know that Whipsaw is dead. I saw the body. Someone beheaded him. King Orange flew into a rage when he learned of it. Do you really know who killed Whipsaw?"

"I did it."

"How is that possible? He has survived dozens of attempts. My mother tried to kill him twice. How did you do it?"

Cleaver looked down. "Dumb luck. Plain stupid dumb luck."

One of the guardsmen said, "Princess, Cleaver is being too modest. Dragon tells a different story. He was there. The way Dragon tells it, Cleaver was brilliant."

"Who is 'Cleaver,' and who is 'Dragon,' might I ask?"

"We leave our names behind when we join the organization. I am 'Cleaver,' because, well, you know. 'Dragon' has terrible breath."

"Dragon said Cleaver took Whipsaw's head off in a single stroke."

"One and a half," Cleaver corrected. "I slit his throat first, and then I cut off his head. It doesn't really count as one stroke like I would kill a cow. I can't take credit that I did not earn."

"You killed one of the most feared men in the kingdom, and you talk about it like you would butcher a cow?"

"Yes, Princess. That is how I thought of it at the time. He was a bull. He would kill me, or I would kill him. He didn't leave me much choice—him or me. Take your pick. I picked me."

"You're a boy."

"I had noticed."

"That's not what I meant. You're big, but you're just a boy."

"Like I said, dumb luck."

"Dragon said he hooked his hand on a tree and flew around the tree. He landed behind Whipsaw and didn't even think about it. He took Whipsaw's head off in a single stroke. Oh, excuse me, a stroke and a half."

"Am I safe in assuming that since neither Bludgeon nor Orange Adviser came back to the castle, they have been killed?"

"Yes, Princess. They are dead."

"Who killed Bludgeon?"

"I didn't do it. I helped capture him, but he died while being interrogated. There was a big fight. Bludgeon died. Orange Adviser died. I helped capture him, too, but I didn't kill him. Bludgeon killed one of our biggest guys in the fight. It must have been horrible. There was blood all over the place."

"So, now what?" Princess asked.

"We wait. King Orange has the next move. If everything went according to plan, your mother is safely hidden away, where she will be difficult to find. Then we find out what he is willing to do to get you back."

Princess shook her head slowly. "You may be stuck with me for a long time."

She helped herself to some of the stew and sat back down on the log.

Chapter 8

Dragon arrived well after dark with the last of the horses borrowed from the wayward guardsmen. Cleaver was on watch as Dragon materialized out of the forest.

"How goes, friend?"

Dragon sat heavily. "It was a bloodbath. The old gardener started to scream as soon as we appeared. He knew we weren't real guardsmen. I got there just as Milady and Queen hit the drawbridge on the way out. Brute had Queen over his shoulder, and she was kicking and screaming. Blade, Stealth, and me stayed at the drawbridge to help the others escape. Brute took an arrow to his back. He dropped the Queen, and she tried to run. Strange picked her up. Stretch and Pug were already dead. They died in the garden. They killed a lot of guardsmen, but they died fighting. Milady, Cheesy, Shields, and Tinker ran ahead of Strange, clearing the path. We all retreated into the woods. Strange took an arrow, but he made it to the horse before he died. Milady and Queen got away on the horse. We left Strange's body there. We left four good men behind. We had no choice. Arrow, a couple of his archers, Cheesy, Shields, Tinker, Blade, Stealth, and me, we held them off as long as possible. Then we ran."

Princess sat beside Cleaver. "Do you really think I could sleep inside with those morons snoring?"

"Forgive me for waking you, Princess. I should not have spoken so loud," Dragon mumbled.

"I heard all of that. You lost four of your men, and you killed a dozen guardsmen for what? Is my mother safe?"

"Yes, Princess, she is with Milady and Cheesy at the treehouse."

"What do you think you have accomplished with this?"

Cleaver said, "We wish to demonstrate to King Orange that he needs to fear us. We wish to stop the rape of the women. We wish to establish a matriarchal basis for the inheritance of property and titles. We wish to put your mother on the throne and make you the heir."

Princess laughed so hard that tears came to her eyes. "What are you? Children? None of this will happen. Mark my words. Men have held power for too long to willingly give it up."

"We have the means to force them," Dragon retorted.

"No, you don't," Princess scoffed. "I will play your silly game because King Orange is searching for a male heir. Once he finds an heir who will be obedient to him, he will kill my mother and me. I can die at the hands of one of his henchmen in the castle, at the hands of a guardsman in battle, or try to leave the kingdom and hope never to be found. No good will come of this."

Princess stood, took a cup of the herbal tea, and went back to bed.

Once Princess had gone, Dragon said, "Milady wants to bring Queen here in the morning. Blade and Stealth will bring her. Queen knows Cheesy from before. Maybe Cheesy can calm her. Milady wants to make this our infirmary. Doc thinks the open air is better for our wounded than the dampness of the caverns."

"There's not much room in the shed," Cleaver observed.

"Cobbler used to come out here with her father fixing the miners' boots. She remembers a stream inside the mine not far from the entrance. She doesn't think the mine collapsed. She thinks it just played out, and they abandoned it."

"How are we to open the mine with no tools?"

"We have tools. They will arrive after dark tomorrow."

"What about our four guardsmen?"

"We give them names, welcome them to the community, and draft them to help clear the old mine. They also need to care for the horses."

"Sounds like a plan."

"WHAT DO YOU MEAN, THEY kidnapped the Queen and the Princess?"

"Your Highness, apparently the return of the bodies at the front gate was a diversion. They entered through the kitchen door and took the Princess and the Queen."

"Did we lose any men?"

"We lost sixteen men, Sire."

"Did they lose any?"

"Four, Sire. Those were all in the group that went for the Queen."

"What about the group that went after the Princess?"

"The four female cooks were so frightened that they reported changing their clothes immediately after the Princess was taken."

"Did they say how many men came after the Princess?"

"They disagree. Between five and eight men came for the Princess. The biggest one threw her over his shoulder and carried her away. A guardsman tried to stop their escape. He was wounded. He said he saw six men, but he thinks some may have been women, Sire."

"How many men came for the Queen?"

"The reports do not agree, sire. It could have been as many as twenty, including the archers who shot from the woods."

"We lost sixteen, and they lost four."

"Yes, Sire."

"Do we know who any of these four dead men were?"

"They were Whipsaw's bastards. They were known troublemakers who we thought had left the kingdom."

"Do we know who led them?"

"Sire, please do not punish me for reporting this. She was the daughter of the noblewoman who was Whipsaw's first rape victim. Unless you kill her, she is the rightful heir to the throne."

King Orange shook his head slowly. "What do they think this is? Do they think this is some schoolyard game? I do not want either the Queen or the Princess back. They can keep them. Bring me the butcher first thing in the morning. He will be my messenger. They will not kill him."

QUEEN AND HER ESCORT walked out of the woods after dawn. Princess saw her arrival and ran to her. "Mother! Are you hurt?"

"No, how are you?"

"I drank some of the herbal tea they make to help me sleep, and I still feel a little light-headed."

Doc said, "Princess, don't do that again. The light-headed feeling can take days to go away. Other than that, have you been harmed?"

"Who are you?"

"I'm Doc, Princess."

"I have not been harmed. Mother, did they tell you why they kidnapped us?"

Queen shook her head. "Complete folly. No good will come of this."

"That's what I said."

Queen looked around, taking in her surroundings. Spotting the fire with the pots, she asked, "Is there any food? I'm starving."

"The hog stew isn't horrible. It's edible."

"Untie me, so I can eat."

Queen was untied. She took some of the stew and sat down on the log. When she was finished with the food, she said, "This can not possibly end well."

"YOUR HIGHNESS, THE captain of the detail you sent after the copper convoy awaits in the lobby, Sire."

"Send him in."

"Captain, I do not wish to hear about your ignominious return to the city. What did you learn of the convoy?"

"Your Majesty, we tracked the convoy to the great river. They must have traveled all day and all night to beat us there. We saw freshly emptied corrals along the way that looked like they were built for oxen. We saw a few dead oxen, but not as many as I would expect for that severe a forced march."

"And?"

"We reached the river and came to a dock. The convoy did not cross the river. There were no tracks on the other side. An old man in a boat shouted that they had gone. They had taken barges and floated down the river. We would never catch them."

King Orange cursed loudly for several minutes. The captain stood silently.

King Orange faced the Captain. "Get out of my sight!"

"Yes, Your Majesty."

THE BUTCHER, THE MAN who had raised Cleaver as his own, stood on the bank waiting for someone to notice him. Scout silently approached him.

"Gentle sir, you are far from home. What brings you to this part of the wilderness?"

The butcher smiled. "You look like my wife. She has been gone for two years, and I miss her."

"You must have loved her very much."

"I did. I have come with a message from the king. He said that if you have the Queen and the Princess, you may keep them. He does not want them back. He said that had you but asked, he would have delivered them here to you. As it is, twenty men died due to your game. He said to not let it happen again. He also said that he takes a dim view of your murdering Whipsaw, Bludgeon, and Orange Adviser. He wishes to see that stop. If you persist in killing his staff and his soldiers, he will come after you. He recognizes that the ambush that took place here was a trap laid by the copper miner. He will not punish you for that. That was business. Business is business, and he understands."

"Thank you, kind sir, for risking your life to deliver this message. We do have Queen and Princess. They are safe and unharmed."

"Might I ask one question?"

"Certainly, sir."

"The last time I saw my boy, Whipsaw was chasing him. Whipsaw's body has been returned to the castle without its head. Do we know who killed him?"

"Yes, we do. He said that it took a stroke and a half to do the job. He seemed to think that was some kind of failure. He should have done it in a single stroke."

The butcher laughed. "Of course, he would think that. Then, he is well?"

"He is, sir. He is instructing us all on the proper ways to dress the game we hunt. We like him very much. You did a great job with him."

"Thank you. I must be off."

"Indeed. Travel safe."

Chapter 9

After four days without contact from the king, Cleaver became impatient. "There must be something we can do to bring King Orange around."

Stealth and Dragon sat across the table quietly eating. They had heard this complaint far too often. Finally, in exasperation, Stealth said, "It's not like we can bring the Queen Mother Goddess of the Forest down to give him a spanking."

Cleaver picked his head up. His eyes brightened, and he smiled. "Yes, we can."

"It was a joke," Stealth cried.

"How do you plan to do that?" Dragon asked.

"Echo Rock. We have to find Echo Rock."

Dragon scratched his head. "What and where is Echo Rock?"

"There is a hollow in the mountains where if you stand exactly in the right place, your voice will carry over the whole city, the castle, and the fields beyond. My grandmother told me about it."

"Where is it?"

"I don't know. I know about where it might be."

"That's helpful," Stealth scoffed.

"I'll go up the side of the mountain where I think it is. You stand on the other side of the city where I can see you. If you hear me clap my hands, you wave your arms."

"That sounds dangerous," Dragon said.

"I've been all through those woods hunting game. I know where to hide if I need to."

Cleaver explained the plan to Milady. She was skeptical, but she approved it. Cleaver, Blade, Scout, and Dragon left to find Echo Rock.

After a half-day of not finding the right spot, Cleaver was about to give up when he stepped on a brittle branch resting on the ground. His companions stationed on the opposite side of the city waved their arms furiously for his attention. He did not see them at first and had moved away from the spot when he noticed Scout trying desperately to get his attention. She pointed for him to go back. He retraced his steps, slowly clapping once with each step. When he reached the broken branch, he stopped. He clapped. He was close, but the echo was not as loud as the snapping of the branch had been.

Frustrated by the difficulty of communicating across the width of the city with hand signals. Cleaver sat and accidentally snapped another branch. His companions went nuts. He had found it. He clapped where he was. They heard it clearly. He lay on his belly and clapped. It was not as loud. He moved a stride to his left and clapped. It was not as loud. He moved a stride to his right and clapped. It was not as loud. The place where the echo worked was half a stride wide, and the person needed to be sitting.

Now they had a plan.

✕

THAT NIGHT, TRUMPET, Milady, Cleaver, and Queen climbed to the location of Echo Rock.

Trumpet spoke first. His voice boomed across the valley so loudly that he could hear the echo bouncing back. "Hear, Yea! Hear Yea! Hear Yea! Citizens of Orange City. Your leaders have sinned. They have done evil, and they must be stopped. The Queen Mother Goddess of the Forest is angry. Hear her as she speaks."

Milady slid into position. "I am the Queen Mother Goddess of the Forest. Your king has performed unspeakable acts. As punishment, I have killed his three henchmen. Whipsaw raped you, and I have killed him. Bludgeon beat you, and I have killed him. Orange Adviser justified the bloodshed, and I have killed him. I will come for King Orange after I have killed his men, one at a time. King Orange, if you wish to live, you will step down from the throne. Turn your throne over to the Queen."

Queen slid into position. "I am your Queen. I am the true descendant of the Queen Mother Goddess of the Forest. Overthrow your corrupt king and return your allegiance to me and rule to the women!"

THE CAPTAIN WHO HAD been forced to lead his men with Bludgeon and Orange Adviser's corpses back to the city waited on horseback at the crossing.

Dragon and Stealth met the captain at the river.

"Top of the morning to you, Captain. What brings you by?" Dragon asked.

"And top of the morning to you, good sir. I never took the opportunity to thank you for sparing my life. Thank you."

"You're welcome."

"King Orange was most amused by your stunt last night. He wished me to tell you that further such activities will result in reprisals."

"Please tell him that we expected that answer. We understand that these things take time."

"I had expected him to be angry when he called me to give this message. He was in rare form. He was in excellent humor. Based on my experience with him in the war, he is at his most dangerous."

"Thank you for the warning, sir. We will be careful."

The Captain turned and rode his horse to the city.

LATE THAT AFTERNOON, the tax collector's horse returned to the stables with the tax collector's beheaded body lashed to it. The tax collector had been visiting outlying farms. All the farmers he was scheduled to visit reported having seen him and having paid their taxes. The satchel with the collections was missing.

That evening, Trumpet, Milady, Cleaver, and Queen climbed to the location of Echo Rock. They repeated the message and added the announcement that the tax collector had been killed.

The following morning, the captain and Dragon met at the same location as the previous day. King Orange was not happy that the tax collector had been killed. He threatened reprisals.

A PARTICULARLY HATED Whipsaw associate was found in his bed with his throat cut.

That evening, Trumpet, Milady, Cleaver, and Queen climbed to the location of Echo Rock. They repeated the message and added the announcement that Whipsaw's helper had been killed.

The following morning, the Captain and Dragon met at the same location as the previous day. King Orange was not happy about the idea that the man had been killed in the castle. He threatened reprisals.

THE FOLLOWING DAY, a particularly hated Bludgeon associate was found in his bed with his throat cut. The room showed signs of a struggle.

That evening, Trumpet, Milady, Cleaver, and Queen climbed to the location of Echo Rock. They repeated the message and added the announcement that Bludgeon's helper had been killed.

The following morning, the Captain and Dragon met at the same location as the previous day. King Orange was not happy that the man had been killed in the castle. He threatened reprisals.

※

THE FOLLOWING DAY, another of Whipsaw's thugs was found in his bed with his throat cut. The room showed signs of a struggle.

That evening, Trumpet, Milady, Cleaver, and Queen climbed to the location of Echo Rock. They repeated the message and added the announcement that Bludgeon's helper had been killed.

The following morning, the Captain and Dragon met at the same location as the previous day. King Orange was not happy that the man had been killed in the castle. He threatened reprisals.

※

THE FOLLOWING DAY IN the predawn darkness, the king's horses were released from the stables. One of the trainers attempted to round up the horses from an open field. He was known for his rough treatment of the horses and was shot with a crossbow.

That evening, Trumpet, Milady, Cleaver, and Queen climbed to the location of Echo Rock. They repeated the message and added the announcement that the abuser of horses had been killed.

The following morning, the Captain and Dragon met at the same location as the previous day. King Orange was not happy that another of his men had been killed. He threatened reprisals.

※

THE FOLLOWING DAY, another of Whipsaw's thugs was found in his bed with his throat cut. The room showed signs of a struggle.

That evening, Trumpet, Milady, Cleaver, and Queen climbed to the location of Echo Rock. They repeated the message and added the announcement that Whipsaw's thug had been killed.

The following morning, the Captain and Dragon met at the same location as the previous day. King Orange was not happy about the idea that the man had been killed in the castle. He threatened reprisals.

※

DURING THE DAY, QUEEN'S two handmaidens, Princess's two handmaidens, and King Orange's personal valet were escorted out the front gate by a group of uniformed guardsmen. There was disagreement as to how and when that happened.

That evening, Trumpet, Milady, Cleaver, and Queen climbed to the location of Echo Rock. They repeated the message and added the announcement that the castle had been penetrated and several servants removed. This was the only day in the campaign that nobody died.

The following morning, the Captain and Dragon met at the same location as the previous day. King Orange had no quarrel with them keeping the women, but he wanted his valet back. Again, he threatened reprisals.

※

A FORTNIGHT PASSED in a stalemate. Every day, one by one, senior members of King Orange's staff turned up dead. Every evening, Trumpet, Milady, Cleaver, and Queen climbed to the location of Echo Rock to announce the day's killing. Every morning, Dragon and the Captain met at the river.

Queen and Princess appeared to have reconciled themselves to their new life, assisting in the infirmary. The abandoned mine shaft was cleared, and a stream was found only a few dozen stride-lengths inside.

An aqueduct was built to divert some of the water from the stream to the horse trough.

With Whipsaw, Bludgeon, and Orange Adviser gone, the wholesale rape of the city's women stopped. The city's men were not as cowed by the poorly trained guardsmen as they had been by Whipsaw and his squad of enforcers, all of whom had been killed in the ambush by the river or subsequently while they slept. The city began to function as a city of its size might be expected to work.

With most of the senior guardsmen who were responsible for training having been killed, training stopped. The guardsmen stood watch, ate, and slept, there being nothing else for them to do. They began to forget what little training they had.

※

THE CAPTAIN WHO HAD been Dragon's contact for the attrition campaign, walked to the edge of the river where the ambush had taken place. He was clad in his britches and his boots but wore nothing else and carried no weapons.

"Greetings, Captain, this is unexpected," Dragon said.

"Greetings, my friend. I have distressing news to deliver. I will deliver it to you so that you know the truth of it, but I must be assured that it is delivered to the lady who commands this force."

"If the news is true, you shall deliver it to her yourself," Stealth assured him.

"The kings we defeated in the great war have regrouped and may already be marching against us. One of my patrols found a family of refugees. They had fled from beyond the great river in an open cart pulled by one horse. They were starving. My men fed them from their field rations. They told us of the army and begged us for safe passage through our kingdom. I had my men escort them to the ford at the west river so that they could pass without having to worry about bandits."

"How big is this army?" Dragon asked.

"The force could be as many as three or four thousand men. King Orange has known for a week. He does not believe this and refuses to prepare. If the army left right after the refugees did, they could be as little as a fortnight away. If they are still camped where the refugees left them, they will need two fortnights. A man on horseback could reach them in a few days. An army moves slowly."

Stealth suggested, "We should send Scout to the ridge on the other side of the river. She might see the dust from a moving army."

Dragon agreed. "We need to take the captain to the treehouse. Milady can meet him there."

Stealth rotated her arm in the air to signal the rest of her squad to come down from the trees. She quickly related to Scout what the Captain had said.

"I will go see what I can see. Bring me a horse and supplies to the Pine Hill mine. If I don't see anything, I'll ride on."

Scout scampered off.

Dragon said, "Captain, we will have to blindfold you. We will do our best to keep you from tripping on things like roots in the way."

Captain nodded. "I understand. I will cooperate. You have had several opportunities to kill me, and you have chosen to let me live. I will see that you do not regret that decision."

✕

CAPTAIN WAS BROUGHT by a circuitous route to the treehouse. Milady met him there. Captain and Milady had traveled in the same social circles before she elected to not hang around to be raped by her father. He told her what he knew of the coming force. The conversation drifted to mutual acquaintances in the city and how they fared under the current administration. Captain asked after the health of Queen and Princess. He was genuinely relieved that they were well. He found the notion that they were assisting in the infirmary most amusing.

After they had talked for what seemed to Dragon and Stealth for forever, Milady said, "Captain, we leave our names behind when we join this band of renegades. I am 'Milady,' and you will be 'Captain' as befits your rank and the duties you will assume as our warrior commander. Your first mission will be training. Our archers are excellent, but they can not wield a sword to fight their way out of a spider web. Most of our people have specialties for which I am grateful, but we need them to do more than they are currently good at. Will you join us as our master trainer?"

"Do I have a choice?"

"Not really."

"Then, I will do it. However, I think I should help plan the strategy and tactics we will use as we face the army that I believe is headed in our direction."

"Done."

SCOUT RETURNED FIVE days later. She met with Milady and Captain as soon as she returned to the south dig site. "The army is between five and six thousand men. They have not crossed the river. They are building a big wooden bridge upstream of the ford. They still have a few days' worth of work on the bridge. I agree that once they cross the bridge, we will have two fortnights before they reach us."

"Thank you for your report," Milady said.

"Milady, that's only half of it." She pulled an ugly-looking iron device from her satchel. "They call this a pistol. It comes in four sizes. This is the smallest. There is a longer version that a small man can carry and an even longer version a large man can carry. There is a much larger version that must be carried on a special wagon."

"What does it do?" Captain asked.

Scout gripped the pistol with both hands and pointed it at a tree ten stride-lengths away. She pulled the lever underneath the body. The force of the explosion knocked her back so hard that she fell to the ground. A large hole opened in the tree, throwing pieces of bark and splinters all around.

The sound of the explosion brought everyone who was inside to the outside.

"The big one can breach the wall of a castle," Scout said.

"How did you get that?" Captain asked.

"I had to kill a sentry for it."

"How does it work?" Milady asked.

"I'm not sure. It has a lot to do with this powder." She held up a small bag. "We need to have Quack look at it. You put some of the powder in the hole here and put this lead ball on top. The spark from this part makes the powder explode."

Captain asked, "Did all the soldiers have these?"

"No, most had the long ones. They have a longer range. The little ones can't shoot longer than an arrow can shoot, but the long ones can shoot longer than an arrow. The biggest ones can hit something from further away. Their aim isn't so good, but they do a lot of damage to what they hit."

"So, how do we fight this?" Milady asked.

"I don't know," Captain said. "We have two fortnights to figure it out."

Queen and Princess had come out after the explosion. "Do we tell King Orange about this?"

Captain shook his head. "He won't believe it. Is there a way we can get the blacksmith?"

Cleaver raised his hand. "We can get the blacksmith. His woodshed is outside the city. He takes a wagon out there every day to get the wood he needs for his fires. Every day he takes wood, and every day the logger brings him more. We can pick him up from there."

Captain stared at Cleaver. "How do you know this?"

"I am the butcher's son. I make the deliveries. Do you think this device is more than Shields can handle?"

"I think we will need all the metalworkers we can get to work on this," Captain said. "Even then, we may not have enough time. Laying siege to a castle is a nasty business."

Milady said, "Scout, you have done well. Take this to our metalworkers. Cleaver, bring the blacksmith to the caverns. Stealth, build a team of lookouts. Watch the road. We'll need all the warning we can get. Captain, Queen, and Princess, we must make some hard decisions if we are to survive the coming battle."

CLEAVER CAPTURED THE blacksmith without resistance. Four archers and a strong young man with a dagger left him with no alternative.

Milady's war council decided that King Orange should be informed of the new weapon. They did not want to risk it falling into King Orange's hands until they had figured out how to replicate it. They decided that since Cleaver and his team were so efficient at kidnappings, they should capture Chronicle Gray. They could demonstrate the device to Chronicle Gray and show King Orange that Queen and Princess were unharmed and being productive in their new home.

Capturing Chronicle Gray was expected to take more finesse than capturing the blacksmith since Chronicle Gray never left the city. He did, however, frequent one particular pub most evenings. The pub was near the city wall. King Orange had allowed the trees in that area to grow higher than was safe. Therefore, getting into the city was not difficult. The team scaled the wall and slid down ropes to the ground. Herbs had given Cleaver a potion to knock Chronicle Gray out. The problem would be hauling the corpulent unconscious old man out over the wall. They considered tying him to a board, running up the ramparts, and tossing him over the parapet to the ground below. They finally decided to tie him to a plank, tie the board to two long ropes, and run the lines over the wall to the horses' saddles. This way, the horses did the heavy lifting.

As they expected, getting into the city was easy. Chronicle Gray was at his favorite seat at the back of the pub. Wearing a stolen Guardsman uniform, Cleaver entered the pub while his team waited outside. Chronicle Gray was chatting with the barmaid when Cleaver sat at the table next to his. He put a coin on the table and ordered a drink. As the barmaid turned away and Chronicle Gray watched her appreciatively, Cleaver stretched his hand to drop the potion in Chronicle Gray's glass. Chronicle Gray caught Cleaver's wrist before he could release the powder.

Chronicle Gray locked eyes with Cleaver. "Have you come to kill me?"

"No, sir. We need you to get a message to King Orange."

"There are easier ways to get a message to King Orange."

"Yes, sir, but not this one. You need to see something. He will not believe anyone else, and you will not believe it without seeing it for yourself. I would not believe it had I not seen it."

The barmaid returned with the drink and took the coin worth much more than the drink.

"So, young man, there is no sense in letting that drink go to waste." Chronicle Gray reached across and drank Cleaver's drink.

After Chronicle Gray finished the drink, he asked, "Are there more of you outside?"

"Yes, sir."

Chronicle Gray stood up, wobbling as he did. "Young man, I appear to have had too much to drink. Could you please escort me back to the castle?"

A few of the patrons turned, but they shrugged and returned to their games.

Cleaver put his arm around Chronicle Gray and escorted him outside.

"How were you planning to get me out of the city?"

"We were going to tie you to a board and use the horses to pull you up. Then we would let you down gently on the other side."

Chronicle Gray shook his head. "Silly boy. Follow me. Your friends can go out on ropes if they wish, but I am not doing that."

Chronicle Gray walked halfway around the city, to the side that would be away from the direction an enemy would likely choose to use to lay siege. He climbed up the ramparts where the archers stood guard. He greeted them as they passed. Midway between two towers, he swung his leg over the parapet and climbed down a vine growing against the castle wall.

When they reached the ground, Chronicle Gray said, "King Orange grows lazy and sloppy. All the vegetation within thirty stride lengths should have been removed."

"How do you know this way, sir?"

"My forbidden library is hidden in a cave in this direction."

"Forbidden library, sir?"

"Yes, you know we used to be a matriarchal society."

"My grandmother mentioned it."

"Ah, yes, the nightly announcements from Echo Rock."

"Yes, sir."

"Technically, the Queen should be on the throne right now. I dare say she would do a better job of it."

"She will be pleased to hear you say that, sir."

"You must never repeat that I said that. It could cost me my life."

"I understand, sir."

By the time Cleaver and Chronicle Gray had reached the horses, the team had collected all the ropes and grappling hooks. They had waited patiently to see if Cleaver returned. They were surprised to see that Cleaver and Chronicle Gray were passionately discussing some political structure ideas that none of the rest understood. The team rode the horses back to the south dig site. Chronicle Gray was blindfolded, of course.

Chronicle Gray and Queen were pleased to see each other. They shared a little gossip while Shields prepared the demonstration. Being heavier than Scout, the kick from the pistol did not knock Shields to the ground. He had placed an armored vest on a post in front of the tree. The shot from the pistol passed through the vest and still made a large hole in the tree.

Chronicle Gray reached out for the weapon. He scrutinized it.

"Is this why you kidnapped the blacksmith?"

"How did you know that? I only took him a quarter-day ago," Cleaver protested.

"My boy, it is my job to know all the secrets. A few escape me, but not many. I have seen enough. Take me back to the city."

As they rode back to the city, Cleaver told Chronicle Gray what he had been told about the four sizes of the weapon he had just seen demonstrated. The team returned Chronicle Gray to the vine he and Cleaver had climbed down. They waited until they saw him clamber over the parapet before they left.

※

AS QUEEN HAD PREDICTED, King Orange believed none of it. He made no preparations for a possible siege. Captain was beside himself with anger. He had fought too hard and lost too many men for him to sit idly by while his commander squandered what little time he had before the army arrived.

Quack and Herbs analyzed the powder and determined its contents. While two of the components were commonplace, one was not. They had enough of that component to make enough powder for fewer than a dozen shots. Even if the metalworkers figured out how to replicate the weapon, there would be no way to fire it.

Abandoning the project, they devoted their energies to building larger and heavier crossbows with more extended range.

Scout returned with the message that the bridge had been completed. The army was marching across it. They could be expected to arrive on the other side of the river in two fortnights.

Cleaver met Chronicle Gray as he sneaked into his library and passed the information. Chronicle Gray was not hopeful that King Orange would do anything about it, but he would give the warning.

※

UNDER MILADY'S DIRECTION, as assisted by Queen and Captain, the renegades prepared for war while King Orange did nothing.

Princess became increasingly concerned for the women and children trapped inside the city when it was attacked. She and Cleaver discussed multiple options at length before deciding on their plan.

Chapter 10

The army took two fortnights to reach the other side of the river. Their camp could be seen from the ridge where the eighty guardsmen had watched the ambush at the crossing. The army took a fortnight to build the bridge a thousand stride-lengths upriver from the river crossing.

Chronicle Gray almost had to threaten King Orange with death to get him to go to the ridge and see the army for himself. Only then did he start preparations while blaming the army's presence on a plot by Milady's people to overthrow him.

Captain estimated the invading army at six thousand. They were well trained, and all were armed with the new weapons. King Orange had fewer than a thousand poorly trained men. Milady had a hundred combat-ready troops armed with inferior weapons plus potentially hundreds of non-combatants to protect. Nothing in Captain's training had prepared him for this. While he kept working on training his forces, he did not want to send them on a suicide mission. He did not know what to do.

As soon as the construction started on the invaders' new bridge, Cleaver, Princess, and their team began bringing women and children out of the city. They were spirited away to hiding places scattered throughout the mountains. They hid in caves and abandoned mine shafts where they had fresh running water and the food they carried with them, if not much else. Each day, small groups of women left the city allegedly to glean what they could from the fields and did not return. By the time the first invader crossed the newly constructed bridge, the women and children were all gone. The men did not notice the departures in their belated panic over the arrival of the invading army.

The invading army moved into position slowly. They knew that they could starve the city out and take it without risking the life of a single of their soldiers. They were apparently unaware of Milady and her troops because they devoted all their attention to setting siege. After the last siege engine had been rolled into place, a man stood out in front of the army. He called for King Orange to surrender. Rather than answer, King Orange's archers responded with a volley of arrows, none of which hit their targets because they fell short.

Queen, Captain, Milady, Cleaver, and Princess watched the activity from an adjacent ridge.

Queen said, "This can not end well."

DURING THE NIGHT, A single of the massive weapons was moved closer to the castle wall and surrounded by branches cut from the forest. It sat, unattended, until shortly after dusk the following day. Under cover of darkness, the weapon's crew hurried to their positions. As soon as they arrived, they lobbed a single ball at the castle wall. It struck the wall a man-height above the ground and did little damage. A second crew joined the first with more cut branches. They placed the branches a couple of stride lengths closer to the wall than the first set of branches. They removed the original branches and put them with the new ones, thickening the barrier. They then moved the weapon closer to the wall. The weapon and its crew were in the range of the castle's archers, but the branches and the darkness obscured the targets.

Another single ball was lobbed against the castle wall. It struck to one side and slightly higher than the previous projectile.

One careful move at a time, the weapon was dragged closer to the castle, and a single ball was fired until the ball hit the castle wall just below the parapet. By the coming of dawn, the weapon had been abandoned, protected only by the branches, and the knowledge that arrows could not damage it.

DURING THE SECOND NIGHT of the siege, eight single balls were lobbed against the castle wall in roughly the same location spaced out throughout the night.

Safely hidden underground, Milady's people were protected from the noise. As Captain explained, in a siege situation, time favors the attacker and not the defender. The repeated small assaults were intended to rob the defenders of sleep. The attacker's camp was far enough away that the noise would not bother the sleeping soldiers. When the time came for the attack, they would be rested, and the defenders would be exhausted.

EVERY NIGHT, THE ATTACKERS lobbed eight carefully timed balls against the castle wall. The wall began to crumble at that point, and cracks could be seen radiating from the target area's center.

On the morning following the sixth night of the siege, Counselor Gray led two dozen haggard men and boys to the south dig site. They arrived wearing only their britches and boots, carrying satchels with the rest of their clothes.

Dragon was the first to greet them. "Counselor Gray, this is a surprise."

"Yes, you are the one they call 'Dragon,' are you not?"

"I am."

"My friend, there are simple remedies for your affliction. Twice daily, rub your teeth with a bit of cloth to remove the build-up from the surfaces, and if you take a stick of straw to poke out the bits of food that get stuck between your teeth, that will help your breath."

Dragon smiled. "You did not come all the way here to tell me that."

"No, I came to repay the favor you granted me by sparing my life. All of the men and boys I have brought with me are related to people in your group. I did not think it appropriate that they should die in the coming siege when I could so easily save them."

"Should I tell Milady and Captain that you are here?"

"Yes, please."

"Your people look hungry. We have a large pot of stew on the campfire. They may help themselves and draw water from the barrel."

"Thank you."

Over the day, Milady's people came and, one at a time collected the men and boys that Counselor Gray had brought with him. The newcomers were blindfolded and taken to be rejoined with their relatives. By nightfall, only Counselor Gray and the man who had raised Cleaver as his own remained.

Cleaver walked out of the woods unaccompanied by any of the people who usually made up his battle group. The man who had raised Cleaver as his own was sitting on the log, staring blankly into the fire. Cleaver gently rested his hand on the man's shoulder. "Father, please stand so I may see that you are unharmed."

The man stood and turned. Cleaver embraced him as tears flowed from his eyes. "Father, I have missed you. I have done many evil things since I left you. Can you forgive me?"

"My son, my only child, there is nothing to forgive. You have acted with intelligence, courage, and determination. From what Counselor Gray has told me, you are a leader and an honorable man. I am proud of you."

"Thank you, Father."

"Many times, I feared for your life. This is far from over. There is much danger ahead."

"Yes, Father. I have been instructed to bring you and Counselor Gray to the treehouse to meet with Milady. Are you in condition to climb halfway up the mountain?"

"I am."

"Counselor Gray, the path is too treacherous to attempt in the darkness with a blindfold. I will trust that you will not betray us."

"I will earn that trust.".

Counselor Gray heard but did not see the escort that accompanied them through the forest to the treehouse. As Counselor Gray observed, the treehouse was so named, not because it was in a tree, but because a large tree had grown up in front of it, hiding it from view. The house was a wooden face built over a cave with its own running, dripping water.

Queen, Princess, Captain, and Milady rose to greet Counselor Gray when he entered the spacious room.

Captain was the first to greet Counselor Gray. "How is the population holding out?"

"Not well. They have exhausted much of the food, and they will run out of water within the week."

"The city will fall in less than a fortnight, then."

"I doubt that city will last a fortnight. King Orange has hidden in his chambers and refuses to come out."

Queen took Counselor's hand. "You are unwell."

Counselor bowed slightly toward her. "My Queen, I am exhausted but not unwell. I have come to you with a plan."

Milady put a plate of bread and cheese on the table. "Please sit."

Princess brought a mug of water.

Counselor Gray sat and tore off a small piece of the bread. "When King Orange went forth and won the great war, I went with him. I have met the generals that I believe are now in command of this assault.

When the city falls, they will burn it to the ground, and kill or enslave all who remain."

He paused to drink from the mug. "They call the new weapons cannons. The cannon can breach the wall of any castle. I have talked to other refugees, and I believe I understand the goals of these new aggressors. They will burn the castle to the ground. They think of it as a haven for rats and disease. They will build their new city at the point where boats can no longer travel upstream. They will build a commerce center there with roads stretching out across the flatlands. While that would seem to work to our advantage, everything they do is based on race. We have no choice but to flee."

"Where would we go?" Princess asked.

"We must cross the far western great mountains. There is iron and coal to build the weapons we will need to defend ourselves when they arrive. The current occupant of the land is a man who uses conscripted labor in the mines. The labor is all men. There are no women. I feel that we can cross the mountains, take him by surprise, and run the mines ourselves."

"How do you know this?" Cleaver asked.

"Since Captain joined you, I have intercepted hundreds of refugees who all told the same story. They think they will be safe in the grasslands beyond the small mountain range immediately to our west. I believe that this army will easily conquer this small range and race across the grasslands destroying everything in its path. We must go further west to the great range beyond."

"There is no passage across the great range or the deep canyon that lies ahead of it." Captain challenged.

"My father was a fur trader and explorer. He was a worthless human being, but he left detailed maps. This map shows a place where the river can be crossed at the end of the dry season. We could then travel to the base of the range, here, and camp in the foothills and cross in the spring. There is plenty of game in the forest on the mountainside and ample fish in the streams."

"Won't they be able to follow us?" Cleaver asked.

"The pass through the mountains is only wide enough for horses in single file. To reach us with their cannon, they would have to sail into uncharted waters to come in from the western ocean. If they found a passage, it could take them years to reach us."

"That is a long walk," Queen said. "We have women and small children."

"Yes," Counselor agreed. "Which is why need the horses."

"Horses?" Captain asked. "How do you intend to get horses?"

"Ah, yes, that is the hard part. Let me walk you through the plan."

The plan was so elaborate that they pulled a piece of blackened wood from the fire to use it to write on the table to keep track of it. All of Milady's combat troops would be involved in its execution. Many of the community's able-bodied non-combatants would take vital supporting roles. When they were done with the discussion, they agreed to implement the plan the next night.

In the darkness, Cleaver climbed to Echo Rock. Shortly after dawn, he clapped his hands three times. He counted to ten. He clapped his hands three more times. He counted to ten again. He clapped his hands three more times. He disappeared into the forest. The signal alerted his cousin, who had stayed behind in the butcher shop, that tonight was the night and that the time was following the third cannon shot.

In the caves, preparations were being made to depart. All the food and cooking equipment that could be carried was put into satchels. Water flasks and skins were filled. Everyone was counseled to drink as much water as they could. Blankets were turned into shawls to protect against the sun. Hats were fashioned out of any scrap material that could be found.

Cleaver and his team left the caves' safety for the pens where the invaders kept their horses at the first cannon's sound. Archer, Bowman, and their teams took positions around the supplies stored at the end of the camp furthest from the castle.

By the sound of the second cannon, all of Milady's people were in place. Cleaver's cousin and three of his friends slid out of the castle and took their positions in King Orange's stables.

On the sound of the third cannon, all hell broke loose.

Archer and his team loosed a volley of flaming arrows into the supply wagons behind the invaders' camp. Their goal was threefold. The first was to destroy as much of the enemy's supplies as possible. Second, create enough chaos to cover their escape. Third, if possible, set at least one of the barrels of the explosive power used for the cannons on fire. Given that the first volley of arrows would reveal their position, they were to only fire one volley as quickly as possible and retreat to join the teams capturing the horses. Bowman and his team, placed on the opposite side of the supply area from Archer and his team, were to fire the second volley choosing targets that had escaped the first volley before retreating into the night.

Cleaver's cousin and his friends opened the doors to the stables and, choosing the fastest horses for themselves, pushed over a hundred of the king's horses out of the stables to the corrals beyond. They opened the gates to the corrals and herded the horses out into the open pastures where Milady's people waited for them.

Cleaver and his team released the invaders' horses and herded them into the open fields. Cleaver killed one of the guards stationed to protect the horses. Dragon killed one, and Blade killed one.

A gratifying, earth-shaking explosion followed by a series of equally powerful explosions testified that Archer, Bowman, and their teams had succeeded in destroying the powder. The horses, panicked by the noise, ran directly into the people waiting for them.

SENSING AN OPPORTUNITY to strike a blow against his enemy, King Orange ordered the drawbridge lowered and his men to attack on the ground. At a ratio of six well-trained invaders armed with firearms against one poorly trained defender equipped with a sword and a dagger, the defenders were promptly slaughtered.

By morning, Milady's people had rounded up all the horses. There were enough horses that all the women could ride. Most of the horses held one woman and two children. Even Queen and Princess carried children on their horses. Many of the older men also rode, and they each took a child. The remaining men and boys walked. The community's most athletic members ranged out ahead, clearing the path or holding back and guarding the rear.

By midday, the invaders had removed everything of value and killed anyone they found hiding in the castle. As night fell, the flames from the burning city could be seen thousands of stride-lengths away.

No attempt was made to chase the fleeing refugees. Historically, few, if any, of the refugees lived to reach their destinations, and chasing them was a waste of manpower. The invaders turned their attention to building a river port to facilitate the plundering of the local resources to benefit the home cities.

※

CLEAVER, SCOUT, DRAGON, Stealth, Blade, and Arrow ran ahead of the slow-moving caravan seeking game and locating places to camp where water and food might be found. The procession walked for six fortnights. At each stopping point, they found forage for the horses. Since they walked the horses at the pace that a man could walk, the horses found the journey relatively unchallenging. Finding feed for the horses was easier than finding food for the people. The water and what food they did find were carefully rationed.

Crossing the nearby mountains was not as simple as Counselor Gray had made it appear to be, but no lives were lost. Crossing the immense sea of grasslands, however, was another matter. The sun was their primary enemy. The random predators or other game they met were quickly dispatched and eaten. They did not lose any of the horses crossing the grasslands.

While crossing the grasslands took its toll on bodies and minds, the nights offered a much-needed respite. Counselor Gray led the elders in his attempt to preserve at least some of the culture's oral history. Counselor Gray was a master teacher and storyteller. He held the children enthralled until the last finally drifted peacefully to sleep each evening. Without his guidance, the journey would have been much more difficult. Baker, Bones, Deacon, and Cheesy also offered wisdom and advice. By the second fortnight of the trek, each of the elders developed their own little following. As each elder passed away, they died in the company of friends who mourned their passing and carried on their teachings.

Cleaver and his father taught those who showed talent in that direction the proper dressing and cooking methods for the game they caught. Cleaver's father survived longer than any of the elders except Counselor Gray. He succumbed less than a fortnight away from the river crossing.

In the last weeks leading up to the river crossing, Counselor Gray, realizing that he would not finish the trek, taught Cleaver, Scout, and Stealth how to read the maps his father had left. On the night Cleaver's father died, Counselor Gray pulled Cleaver aside. "Your father was proud of the man you have become. You will always be a leader even as you seek to return to a normal life. Before we break camp to cross the far mountains, you must choose a wife. I have noticed that you and Blade spend time together and that you are fond of each other. Blade is not one of Whipsaw's progeny. I have researched who among you is and who is not descended from Whipsaw. You are, but Blade is not. I have prepared a list which I will give you before I die. Of all the people

I have come to love on this journey, you are my favorite, and I am as proud of you as if you were my own son."

Counselor Gray lived long enough to look down from the ridge his father's map showed as the access point to the river crossing and see it precisely as his father had drawn it. As he stood there, he knew that he would not be crossing that river. He died during the night before the caravan made the descent to the river's flood plain.

By the time they reached the river crossing, Queen and Captain were the eldest that remained. Cheesy, Counselor Gray, Cleaver's father, Doc, Baker, Bones, and Deacon had all died, as had many babies, primarily due to the heat and dehydration.

The water at the river's widest and slowest point was shallow enough for a horse to walk across it without difficulty. The caravan spent a full day crossing the river and camped on the other side. The plan had been to camp along the river until the spring thaw and then cross the mountain pass after the snow had melted. They pitched camp on a sandy spot near the river and sent scouting parties out searching for game. Scout reported that she had found a large cave a few thousand stride-lengths away that looked like it would be high enough to be clear of the river's spring flood.

The camp was moved to the cave to wait out the winter.

The map showed a second passage across the mountains that could only be used in winter. Two fortnights march further north, one of the river's tributaries froze where it passed through the mountains. This provided passage through which wagons could be brought, and the raw iron from the smelters brought to market for sale. Conscripts would be transported back along the same route.

Cleaver and Captain discussed not waiting out the winter where they were and trying that route. They wondered why Counselor Gray had not suggested it until they discovered the note that the passage was heavily guarded at the gorges. Bands of outlaws demanded tolls for passage. Any invader, including those that had invaded Castle Orange, attempting to cross, would be massacred from above.

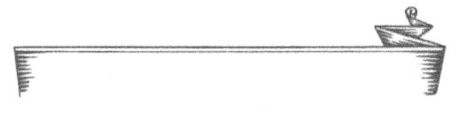

Chapter 11

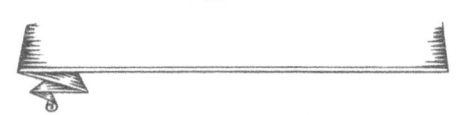

The cave provided protection from the wind and the snow. The fire at the cave's entrance kept predators at bay and kept the cave relatively warm. Every day, barring bad weather, those who were physically able left the cave to chop wood, forage, or hunt. While the food was never plentiful, it was adequate, and the furs provided much-needed cover.

Life in the cave was difficult at best, but it was not without its moments of enjoyment. Counselor Gray had carried with him a trove of books that Cleaver had lovingly protected, dedicating one of the pack horses to their conveyance. Every evening and on the days when the weather kept them from going out to hunt, Queen would read from the books. Captain would sit beside her and tell the stories he had been taught as a child.

Captain's favorite story was the one about the headstrong boy and the giant. The headstrong boy, large and unruly, had become an annoyance to the town's council. A giant had appeared on the edge of the farms and was tearing up crops. The boy was ordered to go and kill the giant. The council expected the boy to fail and be killed by the giant. The boy was gone for a year and the damage the giant had caused stopped. The townspeople assumed the fight had been horrific, both had died, and that was more than they could hope for.

The townspeople were shocked when precisely one year to the day after he had left, the boy, now with a man's full beard, strolled out of the forest with the giant. They wore garments fashioned from the furs of animals they had killed. They laughed as they walked, speaking in some language none of the townspeople understood. The townspeople gathered in the town square. They were not happy to see him, much less in the company of the giant, now obviously his friend, that he had been sent to kill. There was one young woman, unlike the rest, who was happy to see the headstrong boy, now grown to be a man. She ran to him and wrapped her arms around him her tears flowing down her face.

Silently, the boy untangled himself from her arms and dropped to one knee. He kissed her hand and looked up at her, smiling. He took both of her hands and placed one on either side of his face. He stood, put one hand on either side of her face, and kissed her. No words had been spoken, but none were needed.

Together, the threesome sought out a large woman shunned by the townspeople for being taller than all the men. Finding her nearby in the crowd, the giant silently went down on one knee before her. Having just seen the headstrong boy propose to his woman, the giantess smiled down on the giant as he smiled up at her. After the giant kissed her hand, she placed her hands on his face and brought him up to her. With his hands on either side of her face, they kissed.

Without saying a word to anyone in the town, the foursome left. Nobody in that town ever saw them again. The story changed a little with each telling, but all the children could tell the story and understood the lesson.

By the time spring came, most of the refugees were ready to move on. Bowman and a dozen others felt that a valley they had spotted upriver along one of the tributaries would be a good place to establish farms. They did not wish to continue the journey. Once the spring thaw had firmly set in, Bowman and his people left with a dozen horses to establish a new home.

The remainder began the ascent to the pass that would take them over the mountain. The mountain crossing took a fortnight. Two of the horses fell and were lost over cliffs. They were being walked through the pass at that point, and none of the people were injured. The smoke from the smelters could be seen from the last ridge the refugees crossed before making their final descent toward the flat lands beyond the mountain range. There was no doubt that they had found their intended destination.

Queen and Captain descended the final few thousand stride lengths to the settlement alone. At least they appeared to be alone. Milady and her warriors escorted them out of sight under cover of the forest. Too many of the people who had started this journey had not finished it. Too many had been left behind.

The town, such as it was, consisted of a cemetery, a few dozen barracks-style living quarters, a common mess tent, a blacksmith shop, a farrier, a barber, a jail, a saloon, and half a dozen warehouses. The smelters were up the hill adjacent to the coal mine. The town smelled of sulfur. The air was a hazy yellow.

The few men who were out on the street hurried by, averting their gaze. Queen and Captain, dressed in fur garments fashioned from the animals killed over the winter, entered the jail.

The man sitting behind the desk looked up and said, "Your kind are not welcome here."

Queen said, "Where might we meet the man who owns this settlement?"

The man bristled. "I told you, your kind is not welcome here. Go back wherever you came from."

"Clearly, you do not understand," Queen said with the power of royalty. "Direct us to the man who owns this settlement."

Two large men materialized out of the darkness behind the man at the desk.

The man stood, expecting to be obeyed. "I told you to leave. Your kind is not welcome here. Leave before I make you leave."

Captain said, "That would be unfortunate."

No sooner had the last word been spoken than a perfectly balanced knife left Captain's hand and appeared in the man's throat. The knife had been thrown with such force that the bloody tip stuck out the back of his neck. The man clutched his throat. Spurting arterial blood showered the desk as he fell. Unable to scream, he flailed as he grasped at the knife. He dislodged the blade, but in doing so, the serrated edges caused damage on their exit, adding to the damage the blade had done on its way in. With his eyes wide in terror, he took a single breath and died.

Too exhausted to even be angry, Queen stood with daggers in each hand as she faced the two large men. "Now that we understand each other take us to the man who owns this settlement."

Silently, their eyes wide in fear, the two men put one hand in the air as a sign of surrender and, with the other, pointed to the dead man on the floor.

Queen took a deep breath. "No good can come of this."

Captain said, "Who is second in command?"

"There is no second," one of the men said. "He was afraid if he appointed a second, they'd kill him and take everything."

Captain sighed. "Well then, I am about to bring several hundred women and children down the mountain…"

"Women, sir?" the man asked. His eyes lit up.

"Yes, mostly women and children. We have a few dozen men. You will inform the cooks to prepare a meal for them in the mess tent."

"Really, sir, women? Real women?"

"Yes, many with babies. You will tell the men of the town to welcome them with open arms," Captain ordered.

"Single women, sir?"

"Yes."

"Marrying single women?"

"Yes, some with babies."

"Thank you, sir!"

Both men dashed out of the office.

Massaging the pain in her temple, Queen turned to Captain. "You were right, as usual. This was not what I expected, but it was what you expected."

Captain retrieved his knife from the corpse on the floor and wiped it on the man's jacket. "I would have preferred that it be otherwise, but we must always be prepared."

THE REFUGEES FILED down the mountain in groups of three or four at a time under the watchful eye of Archer and his team of marksmen. Cleaver and his team of warriors entered the mess tent first and waited until the last of the people who had climbed across the mountain with them had been seated. The horses were released into an open meadow bordered by a river.

The inhabitants of the settlement, all male, entered the tent in small groups. One of the men who had witnessed Captain's prowess with a throwing knife said, "They're all here."

Queen stood on a bench. "Gentlemen..."

That got a quick laugh. Queen smiled. It was a tired smile, an "end of the road" smile, but it was a smile.

"I was the Queen of Orange until an army invaded and destroyed the castle and the town where I was born and raised. We come to you for safe harbor."

A man in the back stood on a chair and shouted. "If we build houses for the women, will you stay?"

"You will have to court and woo them the same as you would in your native cities. I think many of them would stay. I would like to stay here, and I know that my consort would as well."

Another man stood and shouted, "We don't need a Queen, but we need a mayor. We need a sheriff and a doctor. Did you bring a doctor?"

Queen replied, "We brought two." She pointed to Quack and Herbs.

"Did you bring a dentist?"

Quack nodded.

"Yes. We also brought a butcher, a cobbler, leather workers, metal workers, and weavers. Our baker died on the journey across the grasslands, but the apprentices survived. Many of us are farmers and would build farms in the valley."

Another man shouted, "We haven't been paid in a year. If we elect you mayor, can you see that we get paid?"

Queen looked at Captain, who shrugged. "I don't know. Even if you don't elect me mayor, I will do what I can to see that you get paid."

"I think we should elect her mayor!"

Queen held up her hands. "Gentlemen, none of us has bathed in a fortnight. We would like to take the time to go to the river and wash. Once we have made ourselves presentable, we should come back here and discuss what we should do and how we should do it."

Captain escorted Queen to the river. "Your consort, my Queen?"

"Tell me that you have not thought about it."

"I have, but..."

She put her finger to his lips. "Enough. It is done. Something good will come of this."

Don't miss out!

Visit the website below and you can sign up to receive emails whenever Robert H Cherny publishes a new book. There's no charge and no obligation.

https://books2read.com/r/B-A-HMVJB-KRLZF

BOOKS2READ

Connecting independent readers to independent writers.

Also by Robert H Cherny

Our Last Summer Musical
Stagehands Walk
Second Tango
Flying With Fairies - The Complete Set
Bob's Short Shorts
Cowgirls and Dragons
My Three Warlocks
One Wounded Pilot
Solomon Family Warriors
Rookery Island
Swamp Witch
The Adventures of Doogie Stone
Butcher Boy Rebellion

Watch for more at https://stagewalkerenterprises.com/.

About the Author

Writing has always gotten me in trouble. Still does.I have been a fan of science and speculative fiction since I found it in the young people's section of the library. In grade school, I devoured works by Heinlein, Norton, Asimov, and Huxley among others. By the time I had finished high school, I had read every science fiction book in the town's library.When I was in high school I wrote short stories instead of paying attention in math class. This did not help my math grade and would have serious consequences a few years later.In college, I could be counted on for the divergent opinion. This was after my failed math forced a complete redirection of my life plan. A disastrous Freshman year at Brandeis University, forced a reevaluation of reading materials. Switching majors to theater brought exposure to Shaw, Strindberg, Ibsen, Stoppard, Pinter, Shakespeare, and a host of young would-be playwrights. As a technical theater major, I found that the quantity of material to which I was exposed often surpassed the quality. Too busy to do any writing of his own, I devoted his time to supporting the efforts of others.The Vietnam War brought a tour of duty in South Carolina and the opportunity to begin graduate work at the University of South Carolina. While in the Air Force, my anti-war sentiments did not become an issue, because I kept them secret. I did no writing except for my graduate school classes which I took while still in service. Even here, I was ever the contrarian, unwilling or unable to go where the others went. Fortunately, as a design major, my writing was of less concern than my draftsmanship. The war ended and with less than a month to go on my MA, and no job opportunities in sight, I left school lacking only my thesis and took a paying job at Ringling Brothers Barnum and Bailey Circus World in Haines City Florida Master's degrees in the theater were not worth much in the aftermath of the Vietnam War.Fortunately, through a series of unlikely coincidences, I landed a job as technical director of the then brand new Tupperware Convention Center. At the time, it was the only full-time convention center in Central Florida. I would stay there for twenty years earning an MBA along the way although my work schedule left little time for either reading or writing except for articles in technical journals. My sudden departure from Tupperware provided the time to return to reading and writing...

Read more at https://stagewalkerenterprises.com/.

www.ingramcontent.com/pod-product-compliance
Lightning Source LLC
LaVergne TN
LVHW090126010325
804815LV00002BA/376